8490 £6-00

SIX KEY CUT

SIX
KEY
CUT

Max Crawford

ATHENEUM   NEW YORK   1986

Library of Congress Cataloging in Publication Data

Crawford, Max, ———
  Six key cut.
  I. Title.
PS3553.R293S59   1986   813'.54   85-48130
ISBN 0-689-11778-7

Published simultaneously in Canada by Collier Macmillan Canada, Inc.
Composition by Maryland Linotype Composition Co., Inc.,
Baltimore, Maryland
Manufactured by Fairfield Graphics, Fairfield, Pennsylvania
Designed by Cathryn S. Aison
FIRST EDITION

for JJ
and still I owe you one

There is no real Miami. Not in here.

SIX KEY CUT

ONE

IT was dark and the man in the alley saw nothing but wheels. Feet and wheels. Earlier there had been hands and glasses and long whiskey-slick bars, glistening sheets of wood and black plastic. Before that there had been mouths and faces and eyes, crazy eyes, and glasses caught and bottles held in mouths and other faces and their angry eyes. Before that there had been other men and a woman and something the man in the alley could not remember, some warmth, like the woman sleeping beside him. But now the man saw nothing but feet pressing the sidewalk and wheels scraping the street beyond the alley.

In another part of the city two hunters came for the woman sleeping against the man. One of the hunters walked, the other drove. These two men were young, so much younger than the man they would set after them they would look like boys when they died. These boys weren't looking for the woman sleeping next to the man, they were looking for someone like her, for a type of body—a woman under thirty, no more than five three. The woman they would find with the man was forty, too old, and she was much taller than they wanted, but the boys would be so frightened and hurried when they found the woman they would not notice this.

From a distance one could not distinguish much between the two boys—both were young, one very young—but as they grew near the difference in them became plain. The driver's face was lean, etched and worn. This aging boy's face was deformed by a mirthless smile, his eyes twisted, sardonic at the fear he had caused in the other boy. The walking boy was soft, babyish. His fear had made him characterless, his face a puff of flesh, his eyes dulled by fear. His mouth gaped open, he panted for breath as he walked. In all the nights before this, the driver had led and the boy who walked had followed, but tonight the soft boy went first among the bars and neon and hawkers and hookers and sailors and derelicts and tourists of downtown Miami. The boy went among the scattered drunks, leading the hunt for the woman who would suit their purpose, while the youth in the car followed, smiling at the destructive quest he had set the boy on.

The boy came at last to the alley where the man and the woman lay. He saw them as one dark figure against a trash-heaped wall. He knew before he went to them he had found what they had been looking for. The boy turned from the alley, to walk on as if nothing were there, but the car had come close and the driver had seen his face and the boy's face had told the driver the woman they were hunting was there. The car turned into the alley, its headlights flashing over the man and the woman. The car went past the boy into the alley and stopped. Its light went off. The boy looked back to the street, as if he could still escape, then he followed the car into the alley. The driver set the brake—the boy could hear its grated stroke—and he got out of the car and knelt by the figures. As the boy came forward he saw that the driver had prized the forms apart. The driver took a bottle of whiskey and held it under the woman's nose. He laughed as the woman's head jerked away from the bottle, her eyes opening, staring at nothing.

"Come along, dear, come along," said the driver, laughing, as he fit the bottle into the woman's mouth.

The boy stood back, and the driver cursed him and pulled him down. The boy took the woman by the arm and he and the driver lifted her away from the man and dragged her to the car. The boy opened the rear door and they pushed the woman onto the seat. The boy felt himself stained by the death they were making for the woman.

The boy closed the door on the woman and turned and saw the driver holding the keys before him, the door open, taunting him to get into the car.

The boy shrank from the driver. "Lex, you've got to come with us. I can't do it alone."

"Alone? You've got little Jamie, By dear." The driver reached out and touched the boy's face. He turned his fingers into the boy's cheek and pulled his head down and forced him into the car, under the wheel.

The door was closed on the boy and the unconscious woman, but the boy could not start the car and leave. He pushed the door open. "Lex, don't leave me alone! Meet us at the Cut—please! I can't do it without you—*Lex, please!*"

The driver caught the door and held it. His hand came toward the boy's face, but now he smoothed the boy's hair. "Do you know what will happen to you and little Jamie if you don't die tonight, By dear? Now we have a body for

5

little Jamie, By, and your body is in the trunk and soon you will both be dead and free. Now go, go with God, By, and remember how lucky you are—only the dead are free!"

And the car door slammed and the engine started and the car rolled away. Soon footsteps and the youth called Lex followed and the alley was quiet and dark and the man was left alone. The man knew that these two murderous boys had come and taken the woman from him, but his arms and legs would not lift him to hunt them, not yet, and he was left with nothing but his hatred of them, then even his hatred was taken from him by sleep.

TWO

JAMIE drove fast, faster than she had ever driven before, and still she could not keep up with the car ahead. *Why was By driving so fast?* The speed limit, not a mile over, nothing illegal, not a burned-out taillight, not a missed signal, nothing that would set the police on them—those were By's final instructions, and now he was driving seventy, seventy-five, eighty into the night. Jamie pressed the accelerator to the floor and still she fell back. The night was black, moonless, the road narrow and lonely—these too were part of their plan—but this speed was going to kill her, she could not keep the car on the twisting road, soon the mangrove trees would reach out over her and like monstrous fingers draw her into the swamp.

A light flashed behind Jamie, some dull star passed in the rearview mirror. Jamie searched the mirror but she found nothing there. She was crying now, her tears blinding her. There was no light behind her, there never had been, there was nothing, only some reflection from the dash, some glare from her imagination. She pressed the pedal down, harder. She was fleeing something, but it was not behind her. What she was escaping lay in the car ahead, it lay in what they would do, and she drove faster toward it.

Jamie's eyes flicked from the mirror to the tunnel of light her car bore through the trees. She cried out, for the road was gone. She watched it slip away, its leaden ribbon carving to the left, so slowly that Jamie thought she might reach out and draw it back to her. A bright yellow diamond rushed up from the night, on the sign a black arrow crooked like a broken arm. The car's hood snapped and splintered under the blow from the post. The warning sign raked over the windshield and was gone. Jamie fought the wheel but the car was sliding, its lights cutting across a field of black bars —Jamie locked her hands onto the wheel and flew through the darkness with it. The wheel twisted from her hands, and the car began to pull away from her. Then something, like a giant hand from the sky, took the car and threw it away from the darkness. Something lifted Jamie and dashed her against the steering wheel and there before her again was the tunnel of light and the road and the trees flying overhead. And there, in the distance, were the taillights of the car By was driving. Sobbing so hard her misery came from her like laughter, Jamie set her hands on the wheel and stiffened her leg against the gas pedal and aimed the car toward the sparkling ruby lights.

Jamie had lost the lights again but it did not matter. Now she knew where she was. They had come this way last night—before she had known their plan—she remembered the three-mile straightaway that led to the Keys. There: she could see the leading car entering the mangrove forest above the cut bridge, their destination. Jamie let the car slow— fifty, forty-five, forty—and still the forest and the bridge and the Keys beyond approached with hurtling speed. Her car entered the forest. The road turned left, right, then rose and turned again, and there below lay the bridge and the open sea and beyond the forests of Six Key. The car drifted down toward the bridge, crossed it, and there, on the far side, she left the highway and nosed the car into a grove of trees, a picnic area. Even in the dark the girl could see the tables and barbecue pits placed around, like shrines in a primitive burial ground.

Jamie followed the gravel road till it ended at the bluff overlooking the sea. She turned the car back, to face the highway, switched off the lights and ignition and set the handbrake. She left the key in the ignition switch and got out of the car and walked through the grove to the highway. There she stopped and waited and listened. There was nothing in the night but the surf ruffling against the cut bridge and the rocks of the key. The highway stretched dark and silent into the mangrove forests. No one came on the old highway anymore, not since the freeway to the outer Keys had been built, not at this hour of the night. Still, Jamie waited and listened as she had been told. Then she went out on the highway and recrossed the bridge as she had come and went up toward the low mound of trees where By had parked the car—*her* car—with its grim passengers, the dead woman and the dead man they hoped would pass for them.

Jamie crossed the bridge and walked up the incline to the grove. Once in the forest, Jamie stopped. Panic surged in her. She saw nothing, she heard nothing but the surf below. *By had gone on—this was not the right bridge!* She could not call out or flee or think, she was so afraid. She could only stand in this dark deserted place and wait, as she had been told, and listen.

Now a sound came to her, like that of the surf, but deep in the grove. She went toward the sound—a man's labored breathing—blindly, without hope.

In the back of the grove she found the car By had driven, and heard By cursing, breath tearing from his lungs. She moved silently to the side of the car and saw By toward its rear, near the back door, kneeling over a woman, taking off her clothes, struggling with her dead limbs in the dark. Jamie knew it was By, who else could it be, but still she whispered his name. "By?"

The boy gave a cry and skittered away from the dead body. His voice strangled he was so afraid. "Goddamn you, where have you been?"

"I waited, like you said, and listened, till the road was clear."

"Not for fucking hours! There's nobody on this road, there hasn't been for years, you stupid fucking cunt!"

Jamie moved toward the woman's body spread on the ground. The woman lay on a rubber sheet. "What are you doing?"

The boy's voice cracked. "What am I doing? What the fuck do you think I'm doing?" Then came the abasement she knew when the boy spoke of Lex: "How can he leave me to do this alone?"

Jamie moved toward the woman on the rubber sheet. "I'll help you, By," she said, though she did not think she could bring herself to touch the dead woman. She knelt at the woman's feet and reached toward her shoes, but the boy flung himself at her and pushed her away.

"Don't touch her! I'll do it!" He placed himself between Jamie and the woman's body, and Jamie crept back along the car. There she watched the boy work over the woman, removing her clothes, Jamie thinking numbly that it should have looked as if the boy were making love to the woman, but it did not look like that at all. By stood and Jamie saw the woman was naked. She lay on the rubber sheet, so white in the dark, with shadowy splotches of hair at her groin and under her arms and about her head.

"The clothes," the boy said, and Jamie closed her eyes. "Clothes!" he hissed.

Jamie could barely speak. "I left them in the other car—"

The side of her head exploded. She was on the ground, her head spinning, her face throbbing from the boy's blow. "Get undressed!" he said and began tearing at her shirt. Jamie let the boy undress her as he had undressed the dead woman; there was not that much difference between them, the girl thought as her clothes were taken from her.

The dead woman had been dressed in Jamie's clothes and put in the passenger seat of Jamie's car. Now that that had been done By went to the trunk and lifted the lid. There Jamie could see the wet shine of another rubber sheet, the shroud for the second body. The man who would be By. By reached into the trunk but he could not lift the body out— the sheet was slick, the man too heavy. By called to her— softly now—and she went from where she had been standing away from the car and took the man's feet and they lifted him from the car. By unrolled the sheet and Jamie looked at the man. His head and face were crushed, but even so disfigured, even in the dark, Jamie saw that she knew the man, the detective named Goodge. She sounded like someone far away when she said, "I thought Lex said they were from the morgue."

By held her now. "They are, hon, they are."

11

Now that the boy touched her she realized she was naked. She pulled away from the boy and went into the dark and found the dead woman's shirt. It stank of vomit and wine, but Jamie did not care. She put on the shirt. In the darkness she watched By drag the man's body forward to the driver's side of the car. The woman's body had toppled from its sitting position, sprawling across the seat. By propped the man against the door and reached in and pushed the woman upright. As he did, Jamie saw—and she saw it clearly, as clearly as she had seen the dead detective's face— she saw the woman's arm rise and push against By and she heard the woman speak, mumbling in her sleep.

The woman was alive.

Jamie knelt in the darkness and waited. There was a light from the car. By had struck a match. In its flare Jamie saw the bodies in the front seat, she saw By lean in the driver's door, place the gear in neutral, set the brake and turn the wheels, so that when the brake was released the car would roll onto the highway and down onto the bridge and there be consumed by flames. That was the plan: the car and the bodies would be so badly burned the bodies would never be recognized. They would be thought to be the bodies of By and Jamie. The match died and Jamie heard the splash and smelled the fumes of gasoline. When By came to her he reeked of the fuel.

"Did you put your ID in the car?"

"In my pants pocket. The woman is wearing them."

"One of us has to release the brake and close the door. The other has to throw the lighter in the back, in the gas."

"Aren't you going to kill her first?"

The boy was silent. She thought he would hit her again but he did not. His voice was frail. "She'll die in the crash, in the fire."

"What if she doesn't?"

"I'll kill her then," said the boy, his voice failing.

She drew strength from his failing. "By, we can stop now. We can give the coke back. They won't care. They only want the cocaine, not us. We can take her out of the car and take my clothes and leave her here. The man—the detective—did you kill him, By?" The boy did not answer. "Did Lex?"

"Lex," said the boy.

Jamie stood, to go and take the woman from the car, to undress her and take her clothes, to end it here, and then a glare came through the trees and the ground under her feet trembled. A truck—its motor roaring, headlights probing the dark, its wheels shaking the ground—sprang out of the forest, passing within thirty yards of them, hurtling on down to the cut bridge and Six Key beyond. In seconds the truck had passed and was gone and the grove was dark and silent again. But in the truck's lights Jamie had seen the death car and the bodies in it. She had seen By crouched at her feet, she had seen his terror. She had seen herself in the dead woman's shirt and she had known it was too late to stop.

Then in the dark came a sound, from the car, that she did not understand. A metallic twang, like a bowstring being released; then a scraping, like something being dragged over a grate. Jamie did not know what these sounds meant, but the boy cried out and came to his feet. Then came a crunch, like a footstep on gravel—again from the car—and Jamie saw movement in the dark. The trees around the car were sliding toward them. Then she saw the boy running toward the car and that the car was moving toward the road. The brake has broken, thought Jamie, wildly disjointed, the brake is broken!

The car had moved out on the highway, rolling slowly

toward the ditch, the open front door waving lazily, the dead man toppling, half falling out the door. By reached the car in time to turn the wheel, so that the car would not slide into the ditch but would roll down the highway toward the cut bridge as they had planned. By tried to leap into the car, to reach the brake pedal, but the dead man's body blocked the door. The car was moving faster now and By could only run alongside the car, reaching in and guiding it. The dead man's arms tangled with By's legs as he ran and tried to pull himself into the moving car. The car moved faster now, down the highway toward the bridge, pulling away from By's grasp on the wheel. By leaped at the door, but his feet became fouled in the dead man's arms and he tripped and lost his grip on the steering wheel and fell. By came to his knees and saw the car gaining speed, racing toward the bridge, the dead man's arms and head dragging against the concrete road. The car's acceleration pulled the dead man from the door and he was flung out onto the highway and the car hurtled on toward the bridge. The car swerved, it twisted off the road and crashed, glancing into the bridge abutment. There it teetered a moment, showing its tangled steel underbelly, then slowly it tilted and plunged off the road into the surf beneath the bridge.

"No, no, *no!*" the boy cried out, sobbing, falling forward, beating his fists against the road. The girl came to him, lifting him, comforting him. Then came a noise that paralyzed them—a scream from behind, from the road beyond the grove where they had dressed the woman and prepared the death car. There was another scream—nearer —then a roar from the darkness. A car was speeding toward them, its tires squealing as it left the straightaway and came up through the sharp turns. Now its headlights came cutting through the trees. In seconds the car would be on them, crushing them, discovering them.

By ran toward the cut bridge. He ran blindly, stupidly, with no thought of the girl, of anything, but to run from the death car that lay beneath the Six Key Cut bridge, being washed by the surf.

THREE

THE low clump of trees at the end of the straightaway came up quick, and the fat man in the Buick let off the gas a bit and tapped the brakes and then hit them harder and still the turn came on him at eighty-five. The Buick drifted through that one, crying out, and the fat man lost the beer tucked in his crotch over himself. By the time the Buick got four treads on concrete, the road twisted left, sharper, harder, and at sixty the Buick screamed again and drifted four wheels through the mangrove swamp. Now came a rise, and the fat man pushed it up a bit and flew the Buick over and slid it down the left curve, whooping like a bronc buster.

The Buick hit the dead man—the body that had fallen from the death car—before the fat man knew what it was. The fat man saw the head and arms flapping as the Buick slashed across the dead man's legs, but by the time all this had penetrated—that he had actually killed somebody—the girl had come under the Buick's headlights. The fat man braked and twisted the Buick and missed the girl standing there on the bridge. It had taken the fat man some time to understand he had killed a man, run over him lying in the road, and it took him some time to understand that the girl standing on the bridge hadn't had anything on but a shirt. The first naked woman—near naked—the fat man had seen in years.

The fat man sat in the darkened Buick sweating and gulping air. His hands shook, his eyes burned, he was blinded from the sweat pouring over him. He flailed through the garbage in the glove box till he found his gun. The fat man wiped at his eyes till he could see—till he thought he could see, it was so dark an owl would have sat in his own shit—then he opened the door and got out and went back toward the bridge, the woman in the shirt and the man he had killed.

The fat man stood at the place on the bridge where the woman had stood. He remembered her now. She had been looking over the guardrail. Like she had been throwing something off the bridge, like the broad in that nutty song way back. The fat man went over to the rail and looked down and saw the car on the reef below, being washed by the surf. A man lying in the road, a near naked woman on the bridge and now this car in the waves—the fat man cocked his .45 and started up toward the body of the man. A sound came from behind him—the grinding of a starter motor in a car that wouldn't start. Then the motor caught and headlights flashed on in the trees beyond the bridge and the car shot forward and leaped onto the highway like some wild animal breaking free of its cage. The fat man knew he was a gone fat man now. The man he had killed, he was some kind of friend of the woman in the shirt, and now the woman was coming for him.

In his mind, the fat man crouched there on the bridge, put a two-fisted grip on the .45 and squeezed off eight quick rounds between and a little above the headlights of the on-rushing car. But back in the real world, the fat man flung the gun in the air and waddled along across the bridge at a furious pace. He could hear the car coming up behind him; its headlights cast out his shadow before him, big and de-formed like one of those pinhead giants at the carnival. At the last moment, as the car bore down on him, the fat man threw himself to one side, amid some rubble by the bridge abutment, and the car shot past, missing the fat man by inches. The car went up the highway, into the twisted road he had just come down. The fat man crouched and listened as the car's brakes and tires screamed through the sharp turns. He did not move till he knew the car was not coming back for him.

When the car was gone, the fat man came out and surveyed the wreckage at the bridge abutment. There was twisted steel all about, where the car below had slammed into the bridge before diving into the surf. Part of the wreck-age was a sign that the fat man could not make out in the dark. It would tell him where he was. The fat man snapped open his lighter. Flames shot out. The fat man held the lighter by the crumpled road sign. In its light he read:

SIX KEY CUT

The fat man dropped the lighter, his hand was shaking so bad. What did these words mean? The fat man started backing away, back toward the Buick. This place was crazy —dead men, near naked women, wrecks, killer cars—that was what those three words meant. Even when the fat man got back to the Buick and got it turned toward the freeway and got his breath back and got somebody on the CB, even then, when the trucker wanted his two oh niner, the fat man had a hard time saying those three words. They meant nothing at all to the fat man, except that he wasn't getting off the freeway again, not for a long time, not in this dark, deserted part of Florida anyway.

FOUR

AL'S All-Nite Cigar Store opened at six, the same as the bars in downtown Miami. It was a nice time of morning to be out, thought Al. The streets had emptied at six in the morning and the bars were filled and a citizen could go around downtown and not be mugged or panhandled, a man could walk a block without tripping over the bums and winos and derelicts that littered downtown Miami and plagued Al. Six to about ten was nice downtown, ten generally being the hour when the juiceheads ran out of cash or credit and got eighty-sixed and hit the streets again. By ten o'clock it started getting tough again, the bums coming into the store to pan-handle and shoplift and finger the girlie magazines and threaten Al and his customers and generally be a pain in the ass. These winos were the bane of Al's existence. He hated them with a fury. The only thing Al hated more than these bums was tourists. In their way, tourists were just like the bums. Only worse. The bums might come in and puke on the glossies, but these tourists tried to get inside your head. Stone crabs, blowjobs, the shrimp docks—if Al had been asked where Little Havana was once he had been asked a million times. Al had a sign on the cash register. It read, "I don't know how to get to . . ." and then it listed all the tourist traps in downtown Miami. At the bottom of the sign, Al had written, "But I'll gladly tell you how to Go To Hell!" Al liked the expression on the tourists' faces when they saw that sign.

The broom was Al's weapon against these invaders. Every morning at six, while his assistant, an old black man called Mose, opened and stacked that morning's *Herald*, Al would take up his broom and sally forth against the tourists and the winos and their trash. Garbage, puke, rubbers, crap —you name it, the broom attacked it all, heaving it into the gutter. Not as good as taking the broom to a real wino or tourist, maybe, but for Al sweeping wino and tourist trash off his sidewalk was a close second.

But the broom didn't have too many battles to fight this morning. No real tourists or winos, nothing but grime and dirt and chewing gum, nothing exciting, not till Al got to the alley and saw the sleeping wino.

Al did not usually go down into the alley. No-man's-land. Down there the winos had the upper hand. Once Al had gone off his sidewalk to straighten out a wino on some point or another and the wino had chased Al back up on the sidewalk and into the store and had chased him around the paperback racks till Mose had coldcocked him. After that Al had kept to the sidewalk. High ground. But this morning Al was bored, the sidewalk had been so clean, and he hadn't been chased by a wino in months, and this wino, by the looks of him, was not going to be chasing anybody. By the looks of this wino, he was dead.

"Maybe he is dead," Al cackled and stepped down into the alley.

Al swept up beside the wino and slapped his feet with the broom. Nothing. Al slapped the wino again, on the rear. Nothing. Al began to become concerned but not that concerned. Maybe this wino really was dead. Al turned the broom around and held it like a lance. Al speared the wino's belly with the broom handle. Hard. Then Al saw the eyes—red with hatred, aimed right at him. Al stepped back from the malevolent gaze, but the broom didn't come with him. The wino held it, gripped against his stomach, like a lance stuck in him.

"Hey, gimme my fuckin' broom back," said Al and grasped at the straws. But the broom wouldn't come loose. Al moved in to grab the broom handle, but he saw the wino's eyes, the hatred in them, and he stepped back. "Hey, you fuckin' grapesucker, I'm callin' the cops!"

Al backed down the alley and then he backed up onto the sidewalk and went in the store.

"Goddamnit, Mose, I'm callin' the cops! I mean it! Goddamn wino stole my broom! I'm callin' the cops! What's the number?"

Mose, a white-headed old black man, put down the till and left the store to patch up whatever fix Al had got himself into this time. It was once a week, at least, that Al got into it with some bum or tourist and Mose went out on the sidewalk with the weary patience of a servant diplomat. Mose looked up and down the street. No wino. No broom. He went to the end of the sidewalk and looked down the alley. Nothing. Maybe Al had been hitting the Ripple himself. Mose was about to go back into the store and report the enemy routed when he saw something lying in the alley. A broom with no broom handle. Mose went down the alley and picked up the broom brush. The handle had been broken off down by the binding. Mose ran his finger over the break. Not sharp and level like it had been cut—but close.

"Lord oh Lord," said the old black man. "What devil has done this? What thing has done this?"

FIVE

EXCEPT to run the marathon, Sid Mehring did not ordinarily go above 23rd Street during daylight hours. Then he went on foot, even to visit the unfortunate Mehrings who huddled about above the 70s. This unusual morning Sid left his duplex on East 9th Street and strode briskly up Fifth Avenue. At 48th Street Sid Mehring went east to Madison Avenue and the glass tower that harbored the offices of his maternal uncle, John Grace, an attorney. As Sid Mehring had refused to follow the younger members of the family north into these forests of glass and steel, so had John Grace abandoned those members of his generation who would not toil beyond the sound of Trinity Church bells. Both men were considered individualists by their peers. Sid Mehring was just past thirty, a small man, fit, with a defiant, determined air about him. Many thought he looked something like Bobby Kennedy—irregular features, short tousled hair and a sinewy grin—and Sid cultivated the resemblance, to the point of becoming a rather savage liberal in politics, to the chagrin of the fortunate Graces, who were rather savage conservatives.

Sid entered the glassed tower at 48th and Madison and rode an elevator to a middling floor. There he found the law offices of Goodwin, Phelps, Warne and Minott. He passed a receptionist and went deep into the firm's chambers, running a gauntlet of secretaries whose fingers danced over typewriters the size of Volkswagen engine blocks. Sid did not know how Uncle John and his partners managed it, but there was Jackie, there was Mamie, and there was Lady Bird. Kitten, bangs and twang. And when Sid came upon the inner sanctum, there on her throne sat Eleanor, Uncle John's private secretary, the best legal mind in the office.

The Roosevelt teeth were brought forward for Sid's examination. "Good morning, Mr. Mehring. Mr. Grace is expecting you. Your signature on a few items, Mr. Mehring, before you leave at ten-thirty."

John Grace sat behind an immense polished desk. But for an inkstand and a slender file folder, the desk top was bare. The office was large and empty. Drapes were drawn across two walls, covering the expanse of glass that would have looked out over half of Manhattan had John Grace cared for anything in this place beyond its address. On one of the solid walls, that behind John Grace, hung a photograph of John Foster Dulles. As Sid Mehring cultivated the mannerisms of the Kennedy boys, so had Uncle John adopted the frigid commonplaces of the Secretary. The old man's lower lip was twisted in a scowl, his short gray hair skewered this way and that. He stirred his coffee with his finger and observed Sid with a rancor that belied Sid's being the old man's favorite among the Grace youngsters.

"Sidney," said John Grace: it was his manner of greeting.

"Unc," said Sid Mehring, and John Grace bared his teeth.

"Sit down, Sidney. Some of your munificence has returned to haunt you." John Grace spoke while opening the folder, extracting papers, arranging them about his desk, pressing intercom buttons that allowed subsecretaries to creep in from somewhere, bringing more folders, with more papers to be extracted and arranged in neat stacks. "You recall a man named Simmons, I presume, a Sergeant Simmons, a slain comrade-in-arms, for whose orphaned offspring you established a trust. This girl was but a child at the time of Simmons's death, but has now grown to majority or, luckily, a few days shy of it."

"The girl was Simmons's sister. What's the problem, John?"

John Grace sat back from the desk. "The reason I have asked you up, Sidney, is that the Miami police have called me. Miss Simmons has gone missing under suspicious circumstances. She may be dead."

Sid Mehring had an unfortunate tendency to mimic his mother's family to their faces. He bared his teeth, hunched his shoulders and ran his fingers through his hair, disrupting it. "Tell me about it, John."

John Grace continued with frost in his manner: "The girl's ID and purse have been found in a car that has crashed into the sea. Her body, if she was in the car, has been washed out to sea. It seems the Miami police have begun to speculate that Miss Jamie Simmons may indeed never have been in the car at all, though the vehicle is registered in her name. The absence of a body, and ancillary evidence that the acci-

dent may have been no accident—these and other factors
have suggested that Miss Simmons, for reasons that neither
I nor the Miami police can fathom, has attempted to stage
her own death.

"Logically this should have nothing to do with you or
the trust you have established for the girl. Death shy of
majority: the funds revert to the controlling trust, which is
you. Had she been twenty-one the will we drew up as a
provision of the trust would have devolved the funds to
some group of scrofulous veterans who now oppose the war
they lost." John Grace let a wintry smile rise. "Nothing we
can't handle. The only reason I dreamed of interrupting your
burdensome schedule, Sidney, is that the Miami police are
wondering if you might have been contacted by the girl.
Before—or after—her death."

Sid Mehring gazed at the photograph of John Foster
Dulles. The reflection from a lamp across the room had set
a glowing bulb in the old warmonger's right eye. Sid spoke
carefully, so that he might gather his wits on this matter that
had been scattered far and wide the last year. "The understanding that I would never meet the girl was one of the
provisions of the trust, Uncle John."

John Grace raised a frail silver hand from his lap and
tossed it in the air, as if it might fly free from where it was
attached beneath the cuff. "Yes. But there were the letters
you exchanged, letters I judged a mistake from the beginning. I have always found that letters, more often than not,
lead to some form of physical contact and are often judged
in men's minds, if not a court of law, to be the *result* as well
as the cause of such assignations."

Sid just grinned.

"The Miami police have found evidence in the girl's
apartment that the two of you might have known one
another quite well."

"What evidence?"

"It's this problem you have, Sidney, of finding yourself responsible for acts and events that are now society's concern. Caring for the indigent, the unfortunate, the bereft, even such matters as truth and justice, I'm sorry to say, are no longer the individual's concern, Sidney."

Sid Mehring just grinned some more, and John Grace sighed. He never knew whether the boy was a bolshevik or a vigilante. "Be that as it may, Sidney, even your substantial fortune will soon be depleted if you choose to go on feeding, clothing and educating the families of the men slain while under your command."

"Sergeant Simmons was a special case, John. You could say I wouldn't be here if it weren't for him."

"Sidney, must I be brutally direct with you? You admit you have over the years corresponded with the girl—against, if I may say so, the best legal advice in this town—a correspondence that led to the vile letters you received last year, letters that in my opinion fell just shy of indictable extortion."

"I thought we agreed, John, that those letters were faked crap."

"They are not the question. Or perhaps they are. Did you happen to keep copies of the letters you wrote the girl, Sidney?"

"No."

"Pity. You see, the Miami police have discovered those and other letters in the girl's apartment, letters written both before and after last year's termination of correspondence."

"Other letters?"

"Yes. There are other letters, Sidney, letters written by you, that indicate that you and the girl have had sexual congress."

"Oh what!"

"From her seventeenth year onward."

"This is absolute bullshit, John."

"And that you have supplied her with drugs and further may very well have been attempting to involve her in some drug-smuggling operation. All these letters the Miami police have found in the girl's apartment, Sidney."

Sid rose and went about the large room till Dulles's evil eye was no longer on him. He found himself standing by the curtains, thinking they were a solid wall. He thought if he parted the curtains the city would be spread beneath him, but all he saw was sun-glazed glass and the reflection of his own face on it. "I've never been to Miami, John."

"I thought you hadn't."

Sid returned to his uncle's desk. He sat and began striking the palm of his hand against the chair arm. "I told you last year those Eat the Rich letters I got were phony. Jamie never wrote those letters. This proves it. The pervert who wrote those letters also wrote the ones purportedly" —he grinned horribly—"written by me after the termination of our correspondence. You know, this is beginning to piss me off, John. What was the name of that private eye we hired in Miami last year? I want to get this guy moving again."

John Grace peered into another nest of papers. "Goodge."

"What?"

The lawyer replaced the papers. "The detective's name was Goodge, Sidney."

"Well, I want Goodge back on this, and I want daily telephone reports till he gets to the bottom of it."

John Grace sighed. "You fired Goodge last year, Sidney, when he discovered that your ward did indeed write the Eat the Rich letters, as you call them."

"Did I? Well, find somebody else, John, goddamnit."

"I'm afraid we'll have to, Sidney. A man's body was found near the wrecked car registered to your ward, the car that contained your ward's purse. The man's head had been crushed, either by the fall from your ward's car or from being struck by another vehicle—the man's body was found lying on the highway near the scene of the crash. But upon closer examination of the man's wounds, the pathologists in Miami discovered these misadventures were not what had killed him—the fall or being struck by another car. The man had died twenty-four hours before the crash. Head beaten in by a mallet or some other object with a flat striking surface, though there seems to have been some other cause of death, which I won't go into. In any case, Private Investigator Goodge has been murdered, Sidney, and your ward, Jamie Simmons, is what the Miami police are calling a prime suspect."

Sid Mehring sneered. "Good God, John."

John Grace smiled. "Sidney, you do have an alibi for last Tuesday night?"

Sid opened his mouth and threw back his head. "Have you got a name with the Miami police?"

John Grace did not refer to his notes. "Ashburn. Something like that. Mrs. Sparks will supply you with the necessary details on your way out. And sign some things for her before you go, Sidney."

Sid Mehring walked down Fifth Avenue to the park. He had a Bloody Mary at a local bar and took notes on his conversation with John Grace. Then he went home. He rode the elevator to the top floor. The sound of roller skating came from his neighbor's flat across the way. Sid turned to his more regulated establishment.

The foyer of the apartment was arranged like an office.

Dick, his private secretary, sat behind some kind of Soviet Futurist worker's reading table, scanning the financial papers by the light of a cut-crystal lamp, there being a clash of cultures between Sid's secretary and Sid's wife. Dick did not look at Sid as he stood before his desk grinning. Dick, a lithe young man, raised his eyes briefly, to about Sid's belt buckle.

"There's absolutely nothing in the world happening around here, if that's what you want to know."

"The rink is open."

Dick tossed down the orange pages of the *Financial Times*. "I have told Margot repeatedly that it is absolutely impossible to create profit without some sort of capital movement. I would short gold, Sidney, I am so bored!"

"She's just worried about the election, Dick."

"Oh that."

"Just sit tight, Dick. We'll be moving again in a couple of weeks." Sid tossed his notes on the table. "Transcribe these for me, Dick."

Dick flicked the notes away with the tips of his fingers. "If that's from your meeting with Mr. Grace, you can just as well forget it. He called her as soon as you left the office."

"She didn't call him?"

Dick scooped the notes toward him. "I've told you they are thick as thieves, Sidney."

Sid grinned. "Dick, get me Jamie Simmons's file and that report on Miss Simmons by the Miami private eye—Goodge."

"They're both in the warehouse, Sidney. The Eat the Rich file is here, in the safe, if you want to see it."

Sid Mehring studied the reflection made by the crystal lamp in the blue lacquered wood of the Russian table: the wood and the light were marbled, like moonlight shimmering across a tropical bay. Sid Mehring thought he was imagining Florida, where he had never been, but he was remembering another jungle. "Yes," he said. "That's the one I want to see. Have the other things brought over right away."

Margot Henderson sat in the small library in the back, where Sid and she went when they wanted to escape both business and friends. Books lined the walls, from floor to ceiling, the lighting was low, the color shades of brown and the deep red and green of leather and baize. Two TV sets were placed like gray windows in one wall; in another was a small trophy case containing a deflated rugby ball, a captain's silver bars pinned to the leather. Though there were low chairs about, Margot sat cross-legged on the floor, stacks of books and albums and journals set about her. She wore nothing but large Merthiolate-tinted glasses and a red football jersey. A fringe of sable pubic hair showed from under the jersey. She was quite brown for a Southerner, so Sid Mehring thought; her skin never tanned or faded much. Her lips were full, face flat and round, negroid. Her accent was soft, a slight lisp hidden in it. When Sid entered the room, she was staring into a computer console, a Russian chess magazine in one hand, some book on probability, with graphs and equations Sid did not even like to think about, near the other. A long slender cigarette was stuck in the corner of her mouth.

Sid threw his jacket into the dark and sat so that he could see the market quotes roll by on the computer screen. Margot spoke without looking up. "I've already had the Simmons files brought over—everything but what's in your safe."

"You've talked to John?"

Margot moved the cigarette to a tea saucer. "Dick called him. Poor thing, you ought to let him buy something, Sid. The boy is beside himself."

"I want to wait and see how the election goes. Did John tell you everything?"

"I think so, hon. I've booked you on a flight to Miami this afternoon. We've just got too much going on this morning. Two seats—so you can get some work done."

"Fine." Sid reached for one of the folders.

"Honey, I wouldn't read that if I were you."

"They're just the real letters, Margot. The ones she really wrote."

"I know. Ordinary letters from an ordinary little girl. You've got to deal with the other stuff, hon."

Sid sat back. "Right. Right. Jesus, I wish you wouldn't smoke that crap!"

Margot dipped the cigarette in the tea dregs, switched off the computer console and drew the red jersey over her knees. "Too bad about poor Mr. Goodge, I guess. You know, he could have been the one behind all this, the letters and the extortion."

"Maybe. You got Goodge's report?"

"Yes." Margot held the folder out to Sid.

"What was the name of the boy Jamie got tangled up with?"

"Byron Racicot."

"Rascoe?"

"R-a-c-i-c-o-t. Used to be French a long time ago, I guess."

"Didn't we have some kind of dealing with his old man? What was he into?"

"An old St. Petersburg family—we didn't do much research about that. Ten years ago they moved into some Florida east coast real estate. They had some hard times in the '78 recession. Senior Racicot pushed the family into a shaky public offering. They were undercapitalized and were cannibalized. On the skids the last year or so."

"Anybody we know in the takeover?"

Margot slipped a cigarette from the pack and lit it and blew a stream of smoke out of the corner of her mouth. "You said you wanted a little control over Racicot *père*, just in case."

"Do we still have control?"

"I'd have to look it up."

A door in the book-lined wall opened, and Dick slid through. He held a file, which he handed to Sid Mehring. From beyond the door came the sound of *música norteña* and the smell of tortillas baking and the bored booted stamp of the Polish chauffeur, who, to Sid Mehring's knowledge, never did anything but complain about stomach pains and collect parking violations. Now that Dick had delivered the file he stood in the door, letting in the good smells and sounds. Sid and Margot looked at the secretary, who was not known to dawdle.

"I think I should speak to you alone, Margot."

"Dick," said Sid Mehring, "what is it?"

"Mr. Grace has just called, Sidney. The Miami police have found the body of Miss Simmons."

Sid Mehring tore at the ribbon about the file and let the filthy, forged letters scatter over the floor. "Margot, see how much of Racicot we still own. I may want to nail this bastard."

"I don't think it's the Racicot boy, Sid. I think it's somebody else."

"Bullshit."

SIX

TWO wide roads of concrete met and crossed here and went on toward the horizon. The runways in this part of Opa-Locka Airport, north of Miami, had been abandoned years ago. Grass and weeds grew up between the slabs now, the slabs pocked with holes, cracked, decaying, their surface soft and friable under a film of gray rock dust. Tarmac strips had been laid over the concrete—for maintenance vehicles and ambulances and light plane traffic, anybody who wanted to teach or practice touch-and-gos on the cheap —but they too were warping and sliding away under the wind and heat. Near the intersection of the two abandoned runways was a collection of small buildings, derelict sheds abandoned with the runways. Once these had been maintenance sheds for the old dirigible hangars found in this part of field. These hangars had been large as canyons, three, four hundred yards long, two hundred feet high, torn down for scrap a war or two after the last dirigible had been deflated. Now some of the smaller sheds had been reclaimed, by cut-rate flying instructors, swamp pilots, smugglers, kids who cut every corner they found on the ground so they could stay in the air. In one of these sheds, one a bit better kept than the others, sat two light planes. One of the planes was a late-model Cessna, in good condition; it didn't belong in this gypsy corner of the field. The other plane was covered in black plastic, wrapped and taped, like a fly caught in a spider's web. Only the plane's prop and its wheels were not covered from view.

On the morning that Sid Mehring was sipping a Bloody Mary in a New York bar and writing notes on his conversation with his uncle, a pickup came slowly along the runway of this abandoned Miami airstrip. The two men in the truck were looking into the sheds as they passed, looking for a lost plane. The driver was a tall blond man with a long face, long jaw, long teeth. He seldom spoke but never seemed able to close his mouth, to press his lips together, his jaw was so heavy and his teeth so large. Everybody called this pilot Swede. The man in the passenger seat was smaller, younger, much lighter and quicker than Swede. He wore mirror sunglasses, his hair was clipped short and square, military style, his mouth was held in a tight smile. You could tell Mike was a pilot just by looking at him—at least you could here, on this deserted strip peering into the shaded, dusty gypsy hangars the pickup passed. Mike looked like a man who flew, while Swede, you wouldn't have thought he was a flier even if you had seen him come screaming up MiG Alley in his Phantom, a sidewinder in his tailpipe, flak blossoming around him thick as clover in a cow pasture. Even then you would have thought Swede was a farmer, plowing the sky. Swede looked bored, like he was hunting for a lost bull, as they passed shed after shed, searching for what the two pilots hoped they would never find. The younger pilot, Mike, seemed eager, maybe even excited by the hunt, but that was only because of the way he sat, forward, on the edge of his seat, so he could see past the driver.

The pickup came to the last shed in line, the shed with the two planes in it, slowed and stopped. The two pilots peered at the plane wrapped in black plastic. If the kids had wrapped the prop and wheel struts, Mike and Swede would never have seen the plane. But the prop was stuck bright as a star against the dark cave of the shed.

The two pilots got out of the truck. It was midmorning, hot, still; a heavy colorless sky pressed down on the men once they were out of the air-conditioned truck cab. They walked toward the shed, the heels of their boots pressing sharp holes in the tarmac.

Mike waited outside while Swede went into the shed. The dark made the pilot look like he was working underwater. Swede went to the back of the plane and tore the plastic off the tail. He came forward and tore the plastic away from the cockpit. He then took the plastic from one wing and turned and hooked the plastic over his shoulder and stripped the plastic away, like a slave pulling a barge.

When the plastic had been stripped from the wing, Mike went into the shed. "This it?"

Swede was kneeling, looking under the wing. " 'Fraid so."

Mike turned and looked off toward the field center, the hangars and parked planes, the control tower, the light planes floating about, taking off, landing, drifting through the sky like butterflies. Mike found himself wanting to fly, not like the toy planes in the distance, but really fly. Mike wished he had wings like a bird or anything that could fly or soar or sail. Then maybe he could hide.

    In about an hour the pilots saw two cars on the horizon, one following close behind the other. The pilots watched the cars till they could be seen to be a limousine and a large late-model car. Mike smiled at Swede and held the CB mike toward the driver. "Any last requests?" Swede licked his lips and reached to shut off the ignition and the air conditioning, but Mike said, "Keep it cool, old son. We might pull out of this yet."

    The two pilots got out of the truck and walked a few paces forward, facing the limo and the late-model car. When the limo and the car had stopped and three thick Hispanic men in sharp gray suits had gotten out of the car, Mike walked away from Swede toward the limo. The car looked blind with its dark, dusty windows.

    The rear door of the limo opened and someone within said Mike's name, and the pilot climbed into the rear of the limo, sitting on the jump seat. A man and a young woman occupied the limo's back couch. Another man sat on the other jump seat. In the front, partitioned by glass from them, were the driver and another man, a squat Hispanic like the others. The man in the rear couch was older than the rest, fifty, a man Mike knew as Roberto and a string of names ending with Anza. He lay back in the couch, smiling, talking on the car phone, occasionally pinching the knee of the young woman beside him. Anza's face was narrow and long to look at straight on, flat as a medal in profile, with the graceful beaked nose of the Incas or whatever tribe the Spaniards had wiped out in Colombia or whatever country Anza came from. To Mike the man was an Arab, a sheik without headdress, with his fine manners and perfect English, the silken movement of his hands as he spoke on the phone. Next to Anza sat a pouty ripe Latin girl, maybe twenty, maybe fifteen, it was hard to tell under the rouge and lipstick. The girl chewed gum, biting down rhythmically, with all the animation of a flesh-eating plant. The man in the jump seat next to Mike was named Marcel. Almost as young as the girl, he looked like a novitiate priest, professionally innocent, eager, ascetic, immaculate. Charming and intelligent. Mike had met Marcel twice before. Marcel was a killer.

Anza ended his conversation and handed the receiver to Marcel, who put it away. Anza moved forward so he could see Swede and the three thugs standing around him and beyond them the shed and the two planes, the one still partially wrapped in black plastic. Anza eased back and spoke to the pilot. "Is that our plane, Mike?"

"I'm afraid it is, Mr. Anza."

"Mike, you told me our plane was down. You said you had seen it with your own eyes."

"That was my mistake, Mr. Anza. We flew over the island two hours after the crash—or whatever—and I thought it was real. The boys in the boat got there in the afternoon. But by then they were long gone."

"Mike, why didn't you land and take a look yourself? From one morning to one afternoon can be a long, long time."

"The strip looked real bad, Mr. Anza. Short and beat-up. I didn't want to fuck up the Lear."

Anza smiled and gazed out the window toward Swede, the shed and the planes and the men standing in a loose circle around Swede. "Mike, when are you going to learn to count? The payload could have bought many many Lears."

Mike did not speak.

Anza closed his eyes and pressed his delicate fingers against the bridge of his nose. "How did they do this trick? Did they have confederates on the island?"

"Yessir, I think they did. There must have been more than the two of them—there had to be. It would have taken at least a week to set it up. To get the wrecked plane in from somewhere. The camouflage. And then the incendiary device had to be set off, either electronically from the plane when it landed, which is pretty sophisticated work, or there was somebody there on the ground. The explosion had to be timed exactly with their touchdown. Somebody knew what they were doing."

"Whose bright idea was this, Mike, using the two planes?"

"Mine, Mr. Anza. I'd used it before—Vietnam and a couple times here."

"Tell me how this is supposed to work."

"We'd use two planes, flying pancake, close," said the pilot, placing one flat hand over and nearly touching the other. "There'd be one blip on the radar screen. The mule would drop off to some safe strip and the goat would fly on into here or Lauderdale. Coast Guard would be looking for just one plane and Customs would report the goat clean. They wouldn't even look for the mule."

"And how did this system fuck up, Mike?"

"The mule was flying on the deck, with Swede on top of him. That was the plan. Then the mule developed some kind of mechanical problem. That's what Swede thought. He followed the mule down, saw it attempt a landing on Cay Yerba strip. Then there was the explosion. He made another pass. He saw the burning wreckage, the ID numbers—they matched our plane, Mr. Anza. He thought the kid had bought the farm."

"And Swede didn't attempt to land himself and see for himself that the mule had indeed crashed?"

"We just weren't thinking, Mr. Anza. Not about that. We just didn't think they were capable of anything that sophisticated."

Anza smiled, showing his teeth. "And then Swede, he had just seen a plane crash and burn on that strip, hadn't he? You yourself, Mike, have said the strip looked very dangerous from the air."

Marcel smiled like his boss, but his teeth were better. The *puta* kept working the gum and looking at Mike.

"That would be correct, Mr. Anza," said the pilot.

Anza pushed himself into the couch. He stretched one arm along the back of the couch, behind the girl. "So what happened was that Swede thought he had seen the payload crash and burn, when in truth—in fact—the pilot had landed the plane on this very dangerous-looking strip and he taxied it under some camouflage nets and he or some confederate on the ground set off an explosion in a prefabricated wreckage—an old plane whose wings had been painted with the same numbers as our plane. Is that the way it was done, Mike?"

"Yessir. That was how it was done."

"This must have been a very good pilot, Mike, for this trick."

Mike did not speak.

"Is this why Swede hired him, because he was a very good pilot? Or did he hire him because he was very trustworthy?"

The pilot's mouth had gone dry. Outside, beyond the black glass, everything looked icy and old. "It was the kid we leased the planes from."

"You leased the planes from this boy and in turn you

allow him to fly one? Like we are all boys and these things we are doing, we are all playing with toys?" Anza said something in Spanish, to the girl or Marcel, Mike couldn't tell which. Neither of them made any answer. "Why did you do this foolish thing, Mike? Was it cheaper to lease these planes from this boy than buy them as you should have done? Am I paying you so little, Mike, that you must—what is the English word?—that you must cut corners?"

"It was safer, Mr. Anza. It seemed safer. The planes were clean. It just seemed better than to have me or Swede buy two new ones. We're both pretty hot around here."

"And it was safer to have this boy whom neither you nor Swede knew for longer than weeks, was it safer to have him fly than you, Mike?"

"I thought it would be better to have somebody clean flying one of the planes, Mr. Anza. That way one of us could be working the ground."

Now Mike could see cold forming in Anza. And beside him, Marcel did not move, not a muscle, not a hair. Even the girl had stopped working her fat mouth. There in the cold waste of his failure, just when he thought he had gone free, Mike knew he had said something that would kill him.

"These terms—clean, dirty, goats, mules—they confuse me, Mr. Anza," said the killer. "It would be good, I think, to have a clean flier in a clean plane, Mr. Anza, but surely it would not be good to have a clean flier in a dirty plane and Swede, a dirty flier, in a clean plane."

Mike followed Anza's gaze out the window. The thugs, Swede, they stood as before, the thugs placed evenly around Swede, but now Mike saw Swede had quit. His head was slumped forward, his jaw resting on his chest, his mouth open, his eyes on the ground.

Anza turned to the pilot in the car. "You have told me

why you were not flying with Swede, Mike, and I believe you. Now can you tell me why Swede was in the wrong plane? Was Swede afraid to fly the plane with my cocaine in it?"

"No sir. He must've trusted the kid."

"Ah, there is the problem. It is trust. I trust you, Mike. You trust Swede. Swede trusts the boy. It is such a fragile chain, Mike. You see how it is not broken—this trust—till the last link. That is the way it seems. But in truth—*in fact*—each link before has been broken by this trust. From Swede to you to me. And the breaking of trust does not stop there, Mike. I wish so much for you that I could say it did. But it does not. Maybe there is someone who has placed his trust in me. And now that trust is broken. And who knows, Mike, this person whom I have let down, perhaps now he has let down another. And on and on. That is why I hired you, Mike. I thought you were a man who trusted no one." Anza reached out and touched the pilot's knee with his priestly fingers. "Now, Mike, what do you suggest we do now?"

"We go after them."

"And what is the name of the boy who has stolen ten million dollars from me?"

"Byron Racicot."

Anza sniggered. It was a tasteless thing to come from this man. "Racicot? Felix Racicot?"

"His son. I didn't know who he was when we leased the planes."

Anza sniggered again. "I should hope not, Mike. Ah, it is no matter. It is amusing. Is there anything else we should know, Mike?"

"The Racicot kid had a girlfriend."

"Yes?"

"The girl was in a car wreck, out on one of the keys. It

was her car, her purse was found in the car. They just found her body this morning. Except it ain't her."

Anza began his filthy laugh anew and spoke to Marcel in Spanish, and the pale earnest youth laughed too, a rattle-snake chirr, while the girl remained unmoved, her face as full and polished as the belly of a spider.

SEVEN

THE Miami airport was a madhouse, thought Detective James Ashburn of the Miami police as he strolled toward the Eastern concourse to meet Sid Mehring's plane from New York. And not a figure of speech in sight, smiled Jim Ashburn, supremely pleased that he alone on the force could make such distinctions. The people who came here to flee, those who came seeking refuge, driven by greed and fear and ambition, they were all truly mad. It was the conjunction of Latin America and the Caribbean and the States, the detective supposed. He wondered if the Texas border was quite this crazed. He doubted it. There the madness would be strung along a thousand-mile river. But there was no river here, no distances, nothing to bring some sanity to man's greed and ambition and fear. There was nothing here but a concentration of airplanes and lunacy. And Jim Ashburn fed on it.

Every country, every principality, every Latin potentate, it seemed, had an airline flying into Miami. They were zoo and circus enough. Their personnel, their pilots and stewards and administration, would supply enough smugglers and anarchists and assassins for any freak show. Then came the passengers. Princes of Coke and cocaine; trembling, boasting generalissimos and their staffs and mistresses and families, all waiting to cut one another's throats; the oil spies, CIA spies, Castro spies; the bankers and currency speculators and arms buyers, their tummies plump from money belts, their briefcases bursting with every negotiable instrument printed in Wall Street and the stock exchanges of Caracas and Mexico City and Buenos Aires; the revolutionaries and the counterrevolutionaries, in and out of power, fleeing or infiltrating, *gringo* and *latino*; and then there were the smugglers, not the big-time operators, not usually, just the small fry with a couple hundred grand of cocaine or heroin, every now and then even a bumbling fool with a suitcase of hash or marijuana. Of all the freaks, the Latin maharajas, the sold-out bush pilots, the starlets gone to Bogotá and bad for coke, of all the animals in the airport circus Jim Ashburn thought he liked best these working-stiff smugglers, the self-employed mules. They had been his meat and potatoes for years. He could still spot them a block away. They stood out as clearly as tourists and, at the Miami airport, were almost as common.

Jim Ashburn recalled the last time he had been called to the Miami airport. Six months ago now. The death of the smuggler might have been staged for Ash. Ash had seen the crowd gathered at the exit concourse, heard the screams, the people running into the crowd to witness, those running away for help or from terror. The detective stopped at the place the smuggler had died and smiled. It was a sensitive, refined face, with its gentle smile, the deep brown eyes, so earnest, the trim mustache, so elegant, the sympathy creases about his eyes and mouth—it was not the face of a cop or a criminal. Ash knew his face and adored it. It was so loyal. It had served him so well over the years, as it served him now, as he smiled remembering the poor fool dying the most miserable of deaths, cocaine and blood and vomit and bile foaming from his mouth and anus, his torso bucking in convulsions, his arms and legs rigid, jerking with spasm like a man strapped to the chair. And all for what? Fifty, maybe a hundred thousand dollars. How many condom-filled bags of cocaine could one man swallow? How many could he probe up his rectum before one burst?

Ash had turned away from where the smuggler had died, to go down the Eastern concourse where Mehring's plane was landing, when he stopped and the smile dropped from his face. Ash snarled at the little rodent, the man with the quivering nose and weak eyes and slimy white skin moving on tiptoe behind him. But Ash's face betrayed him for only a moment. Now he had it back—the benign understanding of his partner's ratlike stupidity. Of course Waldy would have followed Ash to meet Sid Mehring. It was why Ash had worked with the white rat all these years. The white rat always knew what Ash was thinking, what he was planning, sometimes before Ash knew it himself. Put Waldy in the far corner of the parking lot and tell him to wait, tell him not to go into the airport for *anything*, and here Waldy was, sneaking along behind Ash in his rubber shoes, coming to watch the rich guy from New York come to Miami to die. What was he going to do without Waldy? Ash smiled, as he turned and blended into the crowd on the Eastern concourse. What was he going to do without his white rat?

                    *   *   *

Jim Ashburn would have recognized the rich guy from New York with a bag over his head, the rumpled suit, jacket slung over his shoulder, the tie pulled open, the worn briefcase, the snapping walk, the tousled hair, the mirthless grin. Ash made his professional smile and stepped forward, toward Sid Mehring. Maybe there was a trembling somewhere in the bad cop, but Ash had it in hand. The fear, the uncertainty would dissolve soon.

"Mr. Mehring," Ash called out and went forward. "Sid Mehring—from New York?"

The tough little rich bastard stopped and looked at the cop. "Ashton?"

"Ashburn. James Ashburn." The cop showed his badge, and the rich man looked at his face. "Narcotics."

"I thought you'd be Homicide. Maybe Vice."

"No. Narcotics for now." Ash smiled and was about to say something else when Sid Mehring took up his briefcase and moved away down the concourse toward the terminal exit. Jim Ashburn went hurriedly after Mehring. The rich bastard spoke to Ash over his shoulder as he walked: "I want to go directly to the morgue. Before checking into my hotel." Mehring grinned. "Or am I under arrest?"

Ash laughed. "You might have been, Mr. Mehring, you might have been indeed if Homicide had gotten here first."

Ash saw Mehring's look turn from him and go sour. Ash followed the look and saw Waldy hustling down the Eastern concourse toward them, from the direction of the main terminal. Mehring looked upon Waldy as some airport freak; he couldn't be a cop. Waldy spun about and joined the two men, rattling away as he went. "You remember it, Ash, you remember the good one we had here six months ago." Waldy turned his tiny pink eyes on Sid Mehring. "Took him twenty minutes to foam out. He was a stuffer, see."

Ash went smoothly between Waldy and Mehring. "Some poor kid, he was trying to smuggle cocaine-filled bags —condoms, if I recall—through Customs by inserting them into his colon. Twenty minutes of fire burning in his belly." They had come to where the smuggler had died six months ago. Ash stopped. Mehring stopped too. Waldy went about the place sniffing. "It's a pity you couldn't have been here, Mr. Mehring, to have seen firsthand the fruit of the business your ward is into."

Mehring hesitated. He started to speak but didn't. Ash liked that. Mehring didn't know. He wasn't sure about the girl. Ash was pleased. It was a beginning. He took the rich man's arm and turned him away from where the smuggler had died. "Can you imagine anyone wanting riches that badly, Mr. Mehring? To die such a death?"

Mal Berger and Jim Ashburn saw each other right away. Amid a sea of cars and scrambling tourists and cabbies swatting each other for the Lauderdale fares and blocks of buses and the yellow haze of jet exhaust, Mal Berger saw the bad cop and his freaky sidekick and the rich guy from New York ease out of the terminal side door. And then as if the little bastard had radar, some kind of homing device, as soon as Berger had spotted Ashburn, the bad cop had looked across the chaos of the parking lot to-ward the two heavy, broken-faced men in the unmarked car and had doffed his hat.

"Fucking faggot," said Mal Berger's partner, a kinder-looking man than Berger. He wasn't a born killer like Mal Berger. The partner, Dan Daniels, spotted the three men sliding into Ashburn's car with his forefinger. "They make us, Mal?"

Berger nodded. "Yeah."

Daniels sat a little higher in his seat as Ashburn's car nosed into the traffic. "That Mehring with him?"

Berger nodded. He moved forward. "Let's see how far this bastard's rope will twist." And Dan Daniels turned the ignition of the shiny crummy Dodge and moved into the traffic after the other shiny crummy Dodge.

Berger and Daniels followed Ash's unmarked car to the morgue. Berger had Daniels park in front. He stood outside the car so he could be seen. Fifteen minutes, then Ash and Mehring and Waldy came out of the morgue by the side door. Berger watched them drive away. Daniels gripped the steering wheel as Ash's car moved into traffic, but Berger let them go. He wanted to see the woman too. The woman these punks had killed for sport.

Berger patted the car's hood, and Daniels got out and the two cops went into the morgue.

Hardy, a good man with a knife, met them inside, and they went along the frigid corridors with all the giant filing drawers. "Hey, Mal, you just missed Ashburn and the geek and this guy from New York."

"No shit," said Berger as they drew up to one of the big drawers and Hardy unlocked it and pulled it back. Daniels stayed back a bit. Dan had killed more gooks overseas than most companies and more than a couple of spics in Miami, behind his badge, but he didn't like the looks of stiffs after they had been drained. But Berger liked Hardy's work. Hardy always made the stiffs look so peaceful, as if they were children pretending to nap.

"It's not her," said Hardy, peering down into the drawer like an artist who's got it right but hates to varnish. "Not the New Yorker's niece or whatever."

"What did he say?"

"That it ain't her."

Hardy started to push the drawer back, but Berger stopped him. "What about her?"

"A wino. Liver big as a cat. Maybe a cracker. She's got the hands and feet." Hardy stripped back the sheet. "Look at that face. Right off a covered wagon."

Berger looked at the face—long, gaunt, the sunken eyes of an old woman. But still, maybe with life she had been young and handsome. Like watching your grandmother for some sign of the passion she had once set off, the stories you heard your uncles tell.

Daniels called out, "Christ, Mal, she's a fucking stiff they picked up. She ain't nobody."

Hardy called back. Their voices rang in the cold, lofted hall, like kids blaming each other for being kept after school. "Hey, Dan, they was all somebody. They had lives. She was a great fuck, you know. Coulda been."

Berger grinned and went to his chilled partner. "Hardy, you got a way with words." They went out into the warm. The cops got to the car, but Berger didn't get in, not right away.

Daniels said, "You want to go after them, Mal?"

Berger got in the car. It was hot. Flesh stuck to everything it touched. Mal Berger liked the cool morgue better. "Not yet."

Ash was enjoying himself now. Having the time of his life. Taking chances. The way he had given Berger the slip at the morgue and now coming back to his office, what they called his office now—it was like shaving with a saber. It was like playing mouse with a tiger. Ash sat behind his desk. It was where he belonged. Like a professor or an exec, he was prince behind his desk. Now he could smoke his pipe. Mehring sat before him, angry, confused. Waldy stood by the window, peering through the venetian blinds, down into the street.

Ash smiled. "As I was saying, Mr. Mehring, I am somewhat of an unofficial greeter. Officially this is a Homicide case. Mal Berger—Homicide—to be frank, Mr. Mehring, Detective Berger wanted to arrest you right away, but I dissuaded him. . . ."

Waldy was good. Mehring hadn't moved. His attention was so occupied with the rodent moving from window to window behind him, he loathed his creeping so, he scarcely thought about the real danger, the gentle concerned man sitting across the desk.

Ash smiled. "You see, I happen to know who your uncle is, and I was able, after a time, to make Detective Berger see who *you* are, Mr. Mehring."

Sid Mehring said nothing.

Ash moved his hand to straighten the file folder on the desk, but he did not touch it. He left it there as Waldy had placed it on the desk. Poor Mehring, with the rodent prowling behind and the folder of filth lying before him, he didn't really know which way to strike.

"But I should warn you that you still might be under some pressure from Homicide. Berger—the Department— they're in trouble. Four indictments this last year. A dozen suspensions. Berger's under siege. He's jumpy. He needs a bust and he needs it bad. Till I was able to convince him that the letters we found in the girl's apartment were forgeries—well, I think he's on another trail for now, but I would watch my p's and q's if I were you. I have been working on the case from the Narcotics point of view for months, but as I told your assistant, Miss Henderson—"

"You've talked to my wife?"

Ash made a bland face. "Yes, of course. I have been in contact with your uncle before"—he glanced at the file on the desk—"about the matter of the letters, and he suggested I speak to Miss Henderson. So much has happened during your flight."

Sid Mehring studied the rotten soft little man with contempt. He put his briefcase on the detective's desk. "You want to trade letters?"

Waldy and Sid Mehring spread the files and the letters onto James Ashburn's desk. For the fifteen minutes they examined the letters, Ash did not touch a single sheet of paper. He had, after all, always had the reputation of being a fastidious man. Now Mehring led Ash through the letters, as if he were a child or an idiot.

Sid Mehring lifted one of the two packets of letters he had brought from New York. "These are the letters I received from Jamie Simmons from year ten till her eighteenth birthday. And this is the crap," said Mehring, forcing a letter from the second packet under the detective's nose, "that started coming last year. You can't tell me the girl who wrote *these*"—he lifted the first packet—"is the author of this filth." He let the second packet drop to the desk.

Ash clicked his pipe against his teeth. "No, no, of course not. But then this private investigator—Goodge—he did report that Jamie Simmons had indeed written these—the latter letters. Didn't he?"

Sid Mehring grinned. "I've got that one figured too."

"Have you?"

"It all fits," said Mehring, now going to the third file of letters on the desk, the letters that Ash—no, it was Waldy who had found them, that was good—the letters that Waldy had found in the girl's apartment, the obscene letters from

Sid Mehring that Ash had forged. "Goodge found out who wrote this crap that is supposed to be from me, and maybe he found out who wrote this other crap, who *really* wrote them, and started blackmailing them. They got tired of paying off—whatever the reason—maybe Goodge just knew too much. Anyway, they kill him and he ends up at—what's the name of the place?"

"Six Key Cut. Well, that's entirely possible, but we think Goodge may have been murdered for an entirely different reason. You see, Mr. Mehring," said James Ashburn, "we are beginning to think that Six Key Cut may be but a small part of a very very big drug burn that's come down during the last several days."

Sid Mehring wasn't listening. He was comparing the letters Jamie Simmons was thought to have written him with the letters Sid Mehring was thought to have written his ward.

Ash turned his gentle, pontifical manner toward the two sets of forged letters. "What we, or at least *I*, don't understand, Mr. Mehring, is the crude, amateurish job done on these forgeries. Not only did the person use the same typewriter, but the language, the obsession with sex—there really is no variance between the girl's letters and the man's letters. No police officer or judge or jury in the land wouldn't have noticed that the same person wrote and typed both sets of letters. My question is this: why go to such elaborate lengths to frame you of crimes ranging from smuggling to statutory rape and do such a hack job of it?"

Sid Mehring looked up from the letters. "The same person didn't write these letters, Ashburn."

Ash gripped the pipe in his teeth. "No?"

Sid Mehring did not take his eyes off the cop. "Same typewriter, but different typing styles. Different errors. Two different people writing identical crap. I'm looking for more than one creep." He closed the file. "I want to go out to the scene of the accident."

"Six Key Cut? Now? It'll be well dark before we get there, Mr. Mehring."

Mehring kept his eyes on the cop. "That's all right. That's when they did it, isn't it?"

EIGHT

IF you wanted to hang supermarket fliers or those little sample boxes or jars or tubes the big soap and toothpaste companies were always handing out to promote some new product, if you were a wino or a bum or a derelict and you wanted a day's work along those lines, there was only one place in Miami you could get picked for a crew—Shu's. During the day and early-evening hours Shu's was deserted, but from about three a.m. to six or so, the hour the man with the broomstick came to Shu's, the warehouse and the streets all around were jammed with men looking for eight, ten bucks a day for nine, ten miles walking and strapping whatever Shu's wanted strapped by rubber bands to every screen door in town.

The dispatcher at Shu's—a man named Leonard, but all the winos called him Shu—had a headache every morning of his life, and the morning the prophet showed up, the kink with the stick, was no different. This morning Shu had not only two hundred winos to get through the day, but one of his best drivers, a fist-happy wop, had been tossed in the slammer for busting up some Cuban dancehall, and Shu was a driver short. And then there was the product Shu had to flog, some kind of dish soap called Snow Bank or something that was proving about as popular as some transparent toothpaste Shu had been told to flog a couple years back. Grin or something it had been called. This dark morning Shu took his head in his hands and climbed up on the box behind the dispatcher's counter and looked out over the crowd of winos huddled around, out of two hundred probably only a handful would make it through the day, and started looking for a sub for the dago who had busted up La Tapatia. It was late, a quarter to six, and Shu was about to call for volunteers among the winos, desperation if there ever was any, you gave these crackers a truck and the five of them, the driver and the four carriers, would be in Tennessee or some godforsaken place by night, when he saw the tall scarecrow standing in the shadows in the back.

The man looked like a ghost, gray, gaunt, his eyes holes in the bad light. In the early-morning dark Shu couldn't see much about the guy, that he was tall and thin, probably a cracker, a Southern boy. They were usually lank and hungry. The dispatcher didn't like these Southerners, they were hard men, mean drunks, but then they were hard workers too, before they got drunk and mean. And most of them could drive a truck in their sleep. Shu called out to the man across the dark warehouse.

"Hey, you! You wanna drive a truck?"

The scarecrow's reply came out of nowhere, not so much loud but so clear, the guy spoke so distinctly, the rafters seemed to ring. "No. I prefer to walk."

The dispatcher couldn't place the accent. Maybe it was a little Southern, a hillbilly who had been in the army, maybe, seen the world. Knew how to speak up. "Hey, Sarge," Shu called out, "what the fuck is wrong with you? I'm offering you twenty bucks a day and you don't have to carry no forty pounds of Snow Bank on your back. I'm offering you the softest job you ever had in your fucking life!"

The reply came clear and reasoned. "Thank you, but I have to walk. There are some things in my mind that need to be worked out. Things that need to be cleaned away."

Shu should have seen this guy a mile off, they were so easy to spot, but it was dark and Shu was so worried about the dago driver he didn't know whether he was coming or going. The guy was one of those preacher/poets. The loonies that were everywhere these days, drifting back and forth across the country, from one slave market to the next, from flophouse to mission to park bench, quoting or preaching or singing their mad sermons and poems and songs about sin or the end of the world or despair over some chippie doing them dirt. That was it, Shu figured, this guy was one of those homegrown prophet types. Even now Shu saw the bake-brain had a long stick with him. Like Moses in Sunday school, with his staff and his rod.

"Yeah? You wanna walk, you're gonna walk!" said Shu. "And you're gonna get shed of that goddamn stick if you're walking for Shu! I ain't taking on no goddamn fairies with their wands! No goddamn witches on their broomsticks! Shitcan the lumber, Sarge."

And the winos all huddled around made some noise, some appreciation of Shu's wit, maybe you would call it laughter.

*   *   *

If you were the dog chained inside the fence or the dispatcher hiding down the street checking on his carriers or the little old lady in the house that sat at the very end of the street, you would have seen the man with the stick coming for you from a great distance. The street was long and broad and straight and from its end it seemed to go on forever. The street was white, the surface crushed shells of some kind, and haze from the heat and the dust from the crushed shells rose and made the far end of the street a shimmering white, as if you were seeing the street through gauze. That was how you first saw the man with the stick, a dark thing moving against this steamy, milky light. The man did not come directly down the street, he went from side to side. He crossed the street as he came, as his black figure grew large, in a stitching pattern, thought the old lady watching from behind her shutters and her door that was chained, from the house that was surrounded by a fence and guarded by the dog. The dispatcher knew the man was working both sides of the street, he was doing the work of two men, maybe three, delivering samples to every house on the street, and the dog knew the man was not a mailman but was someone like him, someone who did not belong on the street. But the little old woman saw the man as an angel of death coming to every house on the street, crossing the road back and forth, like someone lacing a boot, looking everywhere till he came to the end of the street, and then, she knew, he would come over the fence, he would walk past the dog and push back the door and snap the chain, for once an angel of death knew your name you could not hide or buy your life or keep him out by dogs or doors or chains. He would find her there crouched under the table and would scold her in his cold cutting voice and tell her it was time to die. That was why the little old lady didn't use the soap the man left hanging on the fence, that was why she sold it

59

for a nickel. If you washed your clothes in the soap of death, she told the mailman, those clothes would be your shroud.

At the end of the day the man with the stick walked away from Shu's, crossing the scraped field beneath the freeway, going toward downtown and a flophouse and bottle of Thunderbird and a loaf of white bread and maybe a quarter-pound of bologna if he was serious about working tomorrow. That was what the dispatcher thought as he watched the tall dark figure go across the plain. The man's shadow was cast out before him so that as he grew small in the distance his figure and his shadow looked like the opened blades of a pair of scissors that, as the man went away, were slowly closing, cutting across the sandy field of the vacant lot. That was how the dispatcher saw the man the last time he would ever see him. The dispatcher had been around. No matter how good the man was, how hard he had worked, how alone among all the winos he had delivered every box of Snow Bank in his sack and stayed sober as well, no matter that the dispatcher had offered him twenty bucks to come back tomorrow, he could even keep his fucking stick, the dispatcher knew he would never see the man again. It was that look in his eyes, the dispatcher idly thought as he turned back to the empty barn of Shu's, he had seen it before. The man was going somewhere, home probably, and once he got there he was going to set something right. Kill somebody probably. His old lady or the nigger she was shacked up with. The dispatcher would never hear of the guy again unless it was in some squib in the paper, in the back pages where they carry such things— "Vet slays wife and lover with broomstick"—something like that. Even then the dispatcher wouldn't know it was the man for sure. These poor lost bastards, they never got their pictures in the papers, not even then.

The man went downtown. He stood for a while, his back pressed against the wall of a building, looking into the street as the late-afternoon traffic went by. The man was thinking about his aching body and his thirst and his hunger for sleep. These were to be conquered first. His body had to be denied, then his mind—which was split and warring—it had to be unified. This the man did with some power he could not name, some third thing, part body, part mind, but neither. The man did not know what this thing was. Only that it was something other than what he thought or felt or believed or wanted or feared or loved. Once he had heard another man, a soldier, a captain he'd fought with in the jungle, call it Will. The man had listened as the others in the squad had called this thing other things. Without speaking, as the others argued, the man had known this thing was what he was without uniform or insignia or any other sort of dress or rank. It was who he was without a name or family or friends or anyone who knew him by a name. This thing was what he was when he became what he had to do. When the man felt every part of him to be under this control, that he had become what he would do, he pushed away from the wall and went for the things he would need for the night.

The man found a store and bought the things he needed there. He left the store and walked along the street. When he came to a hotel, he went in the door. A clerk sat behind a counter that went alongside one wall of the lobby. The lobby was old, so worn it seemed covered with dust. The light was dim in the room, the glass in the windows overlooking the street brown with age and covered with a black mesh grate. A chair was placed before the window: no one had ever sat there. Behind the counter was a honeycomb of mail slots—empty but for keys to the rooms—no one here received letters. At the back of the lobby stairs led up to other floors. On the wall behind the clerk hung a large mirror, most of its glass missing, the raw boards of the backing frame showing. The mirror—the way the edge of the break curved smooth against the boards of the backing frame—made the man think of a lake shimmering with fresh ice, the fields frozen brown after the fall plowing.

The man spoke to the clerk. "I would like a room."

The clerk took a key from behind him, reaching to one of the mail slots over his head without turning or looking there or at the man. "Five bucks with bath."

The man took the key and put the money on the desk. He took his package and the key and went up the stairs.

The room was located high in the hotel, a corner room with two windows looking out over downtown Miami. The light over the city had grown pink and gray; the signs, the neon that was everywhere, had begun to sparkle like liquid gems stretched in the graceful curves that made them words. The noise of the city—car horns playing, strip-show barkers calling out, tourist buses straining gears—came to the man more gently now that he was in the room above the city.

The man stood before the window for a time, smoking a cigarette. When he saw the light going black over the sea, he pulled the shades over the windows and switched on the light in the room. He undressed and bathed in the rusty tub. He took a thin blanket from the bed and ripped it in half and dried himself with the larger piece of the blanket. His soiled clothes he placed in the tub and ran water over them. He had taken one of the sample boxes of soap from his work, and he opened this and spread the soap over the clothes and washed them, even though he would never wear them again, and rinsed them and wrung them and spread the clothes flat on the bed so they would dry. From his bundle he took out the clothes he had bought that afternoon—shirt, socks, trousers—all dark. He pulled on the trousers and went to the mirror above the basin. He opened a small package and brought out a razor and a packet of blades. He put one of the blades in the razor and snapped it shut. He took the sample soap and made a thick suds from it and shaved with that. That done, he took the blade from the razor and cut his hair around his ears and away from his forehead and eyes. Now his face could be fully seen. The man turned away from the mirror and did not look at himself again.

The man took a small can of polish from the package and tore another strip from the blanket and daubed the cloth in the wax polish and blacked the pair of boots he had bought, the kind he had worn in the jungle, with mesh along the instep. He pulled on socks and the boots and put on the shirt. Now he was dressed in black. He took a watch cap from the package, folded it over the can of polish and put them in his back pocket. He took up the package and emptied the remaining items on the bed. There were a roll of gray duct tape and a few dollar bills and two more razor blades. The man turned to the broomstick he had carried with him throughout the day. He found a place halfway down the length of the stick and took one of the blades and began circling the blade about the stick, the blade cutting deeper and deeper into the wood with each turn. When the blade snapped the man placed the stick across two chairs and struck the cut with the side of his hand. The stick broke into two pieces, each about two feet long. The man discarded one of the sticks. He took another razor blade and went to the blind and reached high and cut off the cord. The man tore strips from the duct tape and taped one end of the cord to one end of the stick he had kept. He wrapped tape around the cord and the stick till they were firmly joined. Then the man raised his trouser leg and taped the weapon inside his calf. He pulled the trousers down so that the weapon did not show. The man took the bills on the bed and put them in his pocket. He looked around the room. All that he had—the damp clothes, the old shoes, the razor and the extra blades, the tape, the small box of soap he had taken—he left as it was. He turned out the light, opened the door and went out into the hall that was as dark as it would be when night came.

For a downtown bar the Firefly was a clean, airy place. Thelma, the night bartender, liked it. She was about alone in liking the Firefly; no other bartender in town would touch the place—night or day. But Thelma was like that. She liked the winos and bums and derelicts and weirdos and all the other trash thrown up by downtown Miami. She even liked the tourists. She didn't mind them. Some of them were sweet, standing there stubbing their toes trying to find some other word for blowjob. As for the others—the winos and weirdos—Thelma could handle them, she let them have a good time. Of course, if one of them ever laid a finger on Thelma, she hit them hard. But this was understood downtown and most everybody treated Thelma with respect, no matter how crazy they got. Thelma hadn't hit anybody hard in a week.

Thelma liked the Firefly during the early evenings, just after sundown, just before dark. A cool breeze came from the sea, sweeping through the open bar doors, as if the Firefly sat on the deck of a ship. The bar was quiet tonight.

Thelma usually liked the quiet at this time of the evening, when it wasn't day, it wasn't night. But maybe it was too quiet this evening, even for Thelma. There was word of trouble going around Miami. That was probably the reason for the quiet. Some kind of killing out on one of the Keys. Tourists spooked at anything these days. Find a couple of Caddies with Puerto Ricans in the trunks—they were headed back to Des Moines. It was like that tonight. Dead. Nothing but one wino sitting down at the end of the bar, sulking over his hangover, nursing a tomato juice. The wino had had a bad night. He had had a bad life. Thelma studied the guy from afar, from down the bar, like she was watching the TV, but she wasn't. That was the thing Thelma liked about tourists and winos. They all had secret lives. Tourists she liked to imagine what they were back where they came from, before they put on the pedal pushers and the slick knit shirts and the sunglasses. She liked to try and figure out what they did when they were real. The winos Thelma liked to study even more. Who had they been before they hit the Tokay? Doctors, lawyers, you'd be surprised how many, professors, too, and all kinds of fancy Dans, just about every type you could think of. That was what Thelma liked about tourists and winos, imagining those mysterious, distant things about them—their homes and the past.

Thelma was thinking about the wino's past, maybe he had once had a home too, when the guy spoke to her. He spoke all the way down the bar. His voice carried. A lot of winos and tourists talked loud and a lot of them thought they were King John, but there was something different in this guy's voice, the tone and everything, very respectful and peaceful, but strong and maybe a little hard. What the wino had said to Thelma was:

"I'm looking for someone."

"Oh yeah? Who?" Thelma went down the bar to the

guy. He wasn't a big man but he wasn't little either. He didn't look tough or mean or any of those things Thelma had no use for. He just looked like hitting him hard wouldn't do him much good. "What's his name?" said Thelma, wiping up ring marks as she came along.

The man turned his head. "A woman. We were in here last night together. Early. She was tall and dark and she was pretty."

Poor bastard, thought Thelma and wiped the bar around the tomato juice. Wino in love. It was the only thing Thelma really didn't like in the study of life. Love. She averted her eyes when she saw tourists holding hands, and to come on a couple of winos embracing—it broke her heart. And here this guy was, this broad had been the love of his life the night before and today he couldn't even remember her name. "I don't know, pal. It's tough. Lotta types go through them doors."

The man said, slow and cool: "I suppose it would be difficult. I looked different last night."

Now the man looked at Thelma. His eyes were like his voice—they meant business. "You're right there," said Thelma. "I ain't never seen *you* before."

The man turned a bar napkin toward Thelma, so she could see what he had written on it. "Does this mean anything to you?"

Thelma looked at the napkin, with the three neat block letters written on it. LEX. Thelma shook her head. "What is it?"

"A man's name. I may have gotten the spelling wrong. I only overheard it."

"Lex? Nah, nah. That ain't no name. Rex. Rex, now that's a man's name. Rex, like the Wonder Dog. You musta heard wrong."

"I didn't hear wrong," said the man and turned the paper back to face him. "Do you have a phone book I could see?" the man said, polite as ever.

"Sure. Yellow or white?"

"White," said the man.

Thelma got the phone book and put it before the man. She checked her watch. "You want another red one or anything? About time for the seven-o'clock news. Don't want to be disturbed. They probably got the latest on that killing —double murder, you know, out there at Six Key."

The man looked at Thelma evenly. "I haven't heard about a killing."

"Yeah, it missed the morning papers but it's been on the radio all day. A man and a broad. Something weird about it. Cops ain't talking. Ho! There it is. Maybe the story has broke," said Thelma, going down the bar toward the TV that had started to make that chattering sound that meant the news was next.

Rudy the cabbie liked murders. He was crazy about them. It was why he lived in Miami. It was why he drove a cab. He liked the danger, living on the edge, being near the front. Miami and a cab—you couldn't get much closer to murder than that. Unless you were a cop or maybe a murderer yourself, and Rudy wasn't either. There were things in Rudy's past that precluded being a cop, and Rudy didn't have the nerve to be a murderer. He didn't have the stomach for it. Rudy admitted it himself, he only liked murder in the abstract. Even when he imagined taking his cab on the sidewalk at fifty or so and mowing down thirty, forty tourists and winos, even then he didn't picture getting his windshield fucked up.

Tonight was going to be a good night for murder in Miami. Not the usual stuff, the Cubans stuffed in car trunks, the fifty Haitians drowned in the hold of an overloaded boat. Tonight was going to be a classic. Rudy had been hearing about it since he got up at three that afternoon. Two bodies found at Six Key—there hadn't been much more than that going around, the radio didn't have shit— but now night was coming on and the evening paper would be out and the paper would have the real story. The slow outpouring of detail, the reconstruction of the crime posed against the investigation by the cops—only newspapers could handle the complexity of murder. Radio and TV were okay for weather and the soaps and stuff about the fucking Russians, but they just weren't up to murder. Murder, you had to read about it to get it all. Rudy parked his bright red cab in the stand by Al's Cigar Store and put his off-duty light on and waited for the murder story to break.

The *Herald* truck came by at seven with the last evening edition, the paper that would be that night's definitive version of the murder. Rudy was out of the cab and onto the bales before Mose could cut the string. Rudy did that and flipped the old coon a half a buck and went back to his red cab. The headline took his breath away:

NEW CUT MYSTERY

And the opening sentence: "Tonight Miami police have released full details of last night's mysterious crash at Six Key Cut." Rudy could have given that guy the Nobel Prize, such a genius wrote that line. Rudy read it all, word for word, not letting his eyes skip forward more than once or twice. When he finished he sat stunned by the grandeur of it all. The murder that had been supposed to look like an accident, the man murdered elsewhere and brought to the scene, the woman alive at the time of the crash, to drown afterward, the staged wreck, the mystery girl, standing naked or near naked on the bridge, and all the theories from lover's revenge to some massive drug operation—the Six Key case was taking on the stature and complexity of an epic. And there was the diagram of the key and the bridge where the car had gone off and the woods where the bodies had been loaded into the death car. And the photos. One of the dead man taken when he was alive. A private eye named Goodge. And the photo of the woman taken after she had drowned, not looking too good. And then there was the picture of the death car's owner, the girl whose ID had been found on the scene. Rudy stared at this girl. He couldn't take his eyes off her. She was so young and so pretty. So innocent-looking. How could a girl like that get mixed up in something like this? There was no way she could be the mystery lady, Rudy concluded, standing on the cut bridge in nothing but a shirt. She was probably dead herself, at this very moment. The killers had commandeered her car, kidnapped her, killed her, left her body somewhere else. Probably. Another murder was the way Rudy looked at it.

"But then why would they put the body of the other broad in the car if they had hers?" said Rudy, and as he spoke he became aware of something. Not a sound, just a presence. Then he looked up and saw the two eyes pinned on his rearview mirror. Rudy jumped. His head nearly hit the ceiling. "Jesusfuckingchrist, pal! You scared the willy-shit outta me! Jesus Christ, pal," said Rudy, groping at his chest with one hand and banging the meter down with the other. "How long you been sitting there? You shoulda spoke up. I coulda had heart seizure. Okay. Jesus," said Rudy, folding the newspaper and putting it on the dash. "Okay. Okay." He went into traffic. He turned a corner. The guy had taken ten years off his life. There he was, making a turn and he didn't even know where the guy was going.

"Okay," said Rudy. "It's okay. Jesus, you are one of the boys who make no noise." He watched the eyes in the rearview. "Okay. Where to, pal?"

A voice came from the back: "I want to go to the Cut. Where it happened."

"Go where? Where what happened? Hey, you ain't one of these fucking—" And then Rudy saw the eyes in the rearview. They had lowered. They were looking at the paper folded on the dash. The words NEW CUT could be seen in the headlines. "Aw hey, pal, all the way to Six Key? You gotta be kidding. That's twenty bucks out there, pal. That's a fur piece. Twenty bucks round trip and I gotta see the color of your money."

Rudy was about to dump the guy when they came to a red light. He took a look at the eyes in the rearview. They had that look, those eyes hanging there from the ceiling. Rudy knew those eyes. Sure, why not ride him out to Six Key? Half-fare maybe. Rudy wouldn't mind visiting the scene of the crime himself. The guy in the back with the eyes, he was just like Rudy. A murder freak.

NINE

THE grove and cut between the keys were as dark as they had been before men came and built the road and the bridge. The man with the eyes stood deep in the grove, the red cab placed even farther back, looking down toward the grove and the curving highway and the bridge and the neck of sea and the dark key beyond. The man was smoking a cigarette, thinking did he dare go down into the grove and walk along the highway to the bridge where they had killed the woman, when he heard the car in the distance, the screaming of brakes and tires as the car came through the twisted road toward the key. The man dropped the cigarette to the ground and crushed it. He went deeper into the grove, where the red cab was parked, and waited.

The unmarked police car came into the grove below the man and stopped. Its dome light sent red and white beams across its roof, the lights slashing through the trees, painting the faces of the two men who had gotten out of the car. A third man, the driver, remained in the car. He kept the motor running, he kept tapping at the brake—the man watching from above saw the ruby lights at the back of the car going on and off, on and off. The two men moved away from the car and the spinning light and went into the dark of the grove. A flashlight played along the ground wherever the men went, so that the man above could follow them, so that he knew they were not coming for him. That the men below had no idea he was anywhere in the world.

James Ashburn spoke as he and Sid Mehring went through the grove, the cop pointing out the tire tracks, the footprints, the gouges in the earth where the drowned woman had been undressed and then redressed in the clothes of Jamie Simmons.

"My opinion is, Mr. Mehring, that someone was trying to set up your ward. That or certainly the most botched body switch I have ever seen. Body switching—faking one's own death for whatever the reason—has been of great interest to me over the years. How often have men killed themselves, if you will, to start anew? Perhaps more often than we might dream, Mr. Mehring.

"Ah, here," said Ash, playing his flashlight about the base of a tree. "Some of Lady Doe's clothes were found here. And over here is where they undressed her. It was all so crude, so clumsy. Not only was the woman quite different in size and age from Miss Simmons, they made no attempts to crush the woman's teeth or mutilate her fingerprints. The sort of things that might occur in a fiery car crash. They even forgot to put Miss Simmons's dainties on the body. Left them here." The flashlight played over the ground.

"The sort of detail I would never have overlooked, had I been in charge of the operation."

"The woman was alive when all this occurred?"

"Yes—alive when she went into the sea. She drowned. Goodge—the PI—he was dead. Had been for twenty-four hours."

A voice came to the two men from the dark. "They kicked a ballpoint in his ear."

Ash stepped back quickly, then stepped even more quickly forward toward his assistant. "Jesus! Waldy! Don't ever come up on me like that again!"

The rat-faced cop grinned. His teeth dripped, he was such slime. "It's the new creepers I got. I move around real quiet now."

Ash gathered his wits. He knocked his voice down to his professional purr. "Yes. Yes. That is how he died." The cop held back a shudder. "They took a ballpoint pen and placed it in his ear and then kicked it into his brain."

The moist, eager voice came from the dark. "The doc missed it at the autopsy the first time through."

Ash turned. They had gone far enough into the dark. Through the trees he could just see the dome light flicking, razor slices of red and white, and hear the crackle of the police band. "Yes. It does indicate that these killers aren't professionals. Someone enjoyed that, I think." They had started back toward the car. Ash looked around him: Mehring walked at his side, but Waldy was not to be seen. Then he felt something directly behind him, someone placing his creepy feet exactly where his had been. Ash whirled around. There was nothing there. No footsteps. Only dark. Off to one side he saw the two men standing, watching him whirl about like a fool. Beyond them Ash could see the car. It seemed to be rolling slowly down the hill, toward the bridge, just as it had happened. Ash managed, somehow, to keep from crying out, to warn them all that someone was in the car, something dead, pushing it down to the cut. Ash recovered. He saw the car wasn't moving at all. He was. He was walking through the trees without knowing he was moving, it was so dark, his mind was so close to snapping from the pressure. All this, the murders, the treachery, the murder and treachery to come, it had made him crazed. He could have sworn there had been someone there, walking behind him, when there was only the dark.

The cops and the rich guy returned to the car. Waldy's ass was chewed there in the light, for leaving the car unlocked, unsecured. Waldy looked around the wild black grove, silently cursing his boss's unfairness. Who the fuck would be out here to steal a car? But Waldy didn't argue. He didn't have the mind for it. His tongue always did a jitterbug when he tried to tell Ash what was right. He got in the driver's seat like he was told. He switched on the headlights and backed the car. Ash and the rich guy went ahead on foot. Down toward the bridge across Six Key Cut. Waldy turned the car and went behind them, the headlights on the two men as they walked down the highway.

Waldy tapped the brake, keeping the car just behind the men as they strolled along. Tap tap went Waldy's left foot on the brake. He didn't have to touch the accelerator. The car rolled down the incline toward the cut on its own. Like the death car had. Waldy watched the two men through the windshield, caught in the headlight glare. It would be so easy to tap the wrong pedal—the gas instead of the brake. A mistake. That was how everyone would look at it. The judge, the jury, everybody would believe him. It happened to everybody now and then. You think brake and hit gas.

Ash wouldn't be chewing Waldy's, or anybody's, ass then. Tap, tap. Tap, tap.

The two men stopped on the highway at the spot where the PI with the ballpoint in his ear had come loose from the car. There were some chalk marks there. Ash was shining the flashlight on the marks, pointing them out to the rich guy, when it was Waldy's headlights that were doing all the shining. Per usual, thought Waldy: Waldy doing all the work and getting zero credit. Ash wasn't so smart. In a lot of ways he was dumb. Wasting the flashlight batteries when the headlights were doing the shining. Not hearing him in the dark. Not figuring out who had kicked the ballpoint in the PI's ear. Even Waldy knew who'd done that. He was pretty sure. What Waldy couldn't figure out was why Ash didn't know. There was only one guy who killed like that. Ash knew that. Why couldn't he put it together? You got a maniac and a guy killed by a maniac. It was two plus two. Even Waldy could figure that out. Lex.

To the man in the grove above, the bad cop and the rich guy were small figures standing on the bridge looking down to the surf. The car and the driver sat on the bridge behind the men, the car's headlights spilling over the empty highway. No one had come this way since they had arrived. Below the surf swept the rocks and the bridge buttress, eating at the bridge and the rocks. The men turned and faced the car. The circling dome light on the roof of the car flashed over their faces, now red, now white. In a short time the men went to the car, one ceremoniously opening the door for the other. Both sat in the back. The driver pulled the car across the bridge into the grove on the next key and turned around. The car then came back across the bridge and up toward the grove where the man stood in the dark watching them. The car followed the highway, turning, its headlights raking the trees above the man's head, and was gone but for the sound of its motor straining through the sharp curves. Then there was silence and the key and the grove were dark.

Now that the car was gone, the man flashed open a lighter he had found in the cab and lit a cigarette. In the light he could see the smooth red bulk of the cab, parked back in the trees. One of the cab's rear doors stood open. The trunk lid was open too. The man put the lighter in his pocket and went to the cab. He closed the door. He went to the back of the car, to the open trunk. Inside the trunk lay a form covered by a tarpaulin. The man reached in and fitted the tarp around the form—a human figure—and closed the trunk lid. He went forward and opened the driver's door and slid under the wheel. He adjusted the seat and worked the gears and looked about inside the cab before he started the motor. When all this was done, he took a slip of paper from one pocket and the lighter from the other. He struck the lighter and looked at the paper in the light. It was a page from a telephone book. The man saw that he remembered the address printed after the name Lexington and then he held the flame to the paper and watched it burn to his fingers. He dropped the flaming paper out the window. He took up the newspaper from the dash and opened it and struck the lighter again. He held the flame near the open page, first near the photograph of the dead man, then near that of the drowned woman. Then he held the flame near the picture of the missing girl. The flame first browned, then made black, then licked out and ate away the face of Jamie Simmons.

TEN

THE cops let Sid Mehring off at a hotel near downtown. Sid watched the unmarked car disappear into the evening traffic, then he went into the hotel, checked in and was shown to his room. He went to the phone and dialed New York. Dick came on the line, then in seconds he heard Margot's voice. Sid spoke to them both, telling them what he had learned.

"It looks like the two of them, Jamie and this boy-friend, were involved in some kind of drug burn—

—No, no, that's not important.

—Margot, it's too complicated and it's irrelevant. Faked planes. Faked crashes. And now the faked deaths.

—That's right. The man who was to be Jamie's boy-friend was Goodge and the woman who was to be Jamie—nobody knows who she was. A derelict.

—No, the woman wasn't dead.

—Right. Murder.

—No, Margot, we don't know it was Jamie. Not for sure.

—Yes. It would seem that the two of them had something to do with it, but we don't know that.

—Jesus, would the two of you shut up! I can't hear myself think.

—Yeah. Yeah. Right. I know. It's a tea party now. Me, the cops and the Colombians. I just hope the hell I get there first. Listen, one of the slimes they got for cops down here told me a good one. You know how these Colombians kill people who rip them off? They take a pipe and shove it up a guy's ass and they put a rat in the pipe and cap it and then they heat the free end of the pipe with a blowtorch and the rat eats his way up right out the guy's mouth.

—Just what the cops told me." Sid Mehring laughed.

"Yeah. Byron Racicot.

—Yeah, right. Son of the blueblood we bought out. Felix Racicot. Son Byron was the leader of some sort of gang in high school—Beach High—dealing drugs, the usual. Then this gang moved into smuggling. They were all rich and had boats. That's when they got hooked up with what they got for a mob down here. But it was still marijuana, still no Colombians. That came with cocaine.

—Cocaine's big, big money. Very compact. You can fit a million bucks in an attaché case.

—They're using the figure ten million, but it could be a lot more.

—No, I think they had somebody working with them. It's too heavy for two kids. Still, the Racicot kid is a hot pilot. So the cops say.

—They've got a line on two ex-navy pilots, but Ash—the cop—wasn't talking. And there was somebody else. Somebody named Lex. Lexington, I gather. This cop Ash seems to think this Lex might be our letter writer.

—Maybe. I still think the Racicot kid is behind it all.

—Lexington."

Sid looked at his watch. His room was high in the hotel tower, looking east toward the sea. It was night there now and the lights from a fishing fleet blinked like stars set in line. Sid turned back to the phone.

"Look, Margot, one of the few things I know is that people never really change. An old bastard was a baby bastard. The current Jamie Simmons is still the girl I knew as Sergeant Simmons's sister, and someone, either this boyfriend or his sidekick, is framing her for murder.

—So I'm a fool.

—No, Margot, I don't want you coming down here. It's too strange. Too dangerous.

—Yes, I love you too.

—No, no, I'm letting the cops handle this. Look, the only thing I want to do is to drop by Jamie's apartment. That's all.

—Yeah, you're right. We should get a new PI on this.

—I'll find somebody first thing in the morning. Promise. I'll work through the cops and this guy.

—No, no. I've learned my lesson. No Sam Spade stuff.

—I'll call you in the morning.

—All right, darling. Talk to you tomorrow. Bye-bye.

—Me too."

Sid put down the receiver. He stood and stretched. He went to the dressing room and took off his suit, shirt and tie and pulled on slacks, knit shirt and running shoes. From his wallet he took his New York driver's license, a telephone credit card and twenty hundred-dollar bills and a few odd twenties and tens. These he placed loose in his pocket. He pulled on a dark green windbreaker and looked in the mirror. Another tourist. He went out.

ELEVEN

AN unmarked car moved easily through darkening city streets. The two men in the car, Waldy and Ash, did not speak. Waldy looked at it all as they passed—at every pedestrian, into every car, up every alley—for something happening or about to happen. Even for something that was over. Waldy looked for action, anything, just some violence or crime. A crazy praying on his knees on a street corner would be okay. Anything to break the calm. But the city offered nothing tonight. No tourists, that was part of it. The wrong time of the year for tourists, though Waldy forgot what time of year it was from time to time. But it was more than the tourists bailing out. The city was deader than that. Maybe a hurricane was coming in. Waldy didn't pay much attention to weather, maybe even less than to the seasons of the year. Waldy looked out at the people slouching by. No storm tonight, but maybe one was coming on. That was why everybody was so lifeless, the city so dead. The quiet before the storm.

Waldy glanced at his partner, Ash. Ash looked as dead as the streets. Usually Ash was like a heeled dog when they drove through the city. Straining, watching, thinking, *wanting* it to happen. But not tonight. There he sat, slumped into the seat, head low, gazing out the window, seeing nothing. Maybe it was the storm coming, the one nobody had seen yet, it wasn't even on the radar screen. And maybe, thought Waldy, there was a storm coming in Ash. Maybe that was why Ash looked so dead. Now Waldy understood it. It was Lex. After all these years of letting that maniac run loose, after all the times Ash had pulled that freak's bacon out of the fire—now Ash was turning on him. Waldy should have seen it sooner. The way Ash had dropped the freak's name to the rich guy. It had come out like an accident. But maybe it wasn't an accident. Maybe Ash was setting up Lex with the rich guy. Maybe Ash was thinking about going all the way. Waldy steered the car at a wino who crossed against the light. Ash didn't even notice, even with the wino screaming he was going to cut the cop's heart out. Waldy knew it now. After all these years Ash was going to turn on his boyfriend. That was the storm coming.

The unmarked car turned down the ramp into the garage under the police headquarters. Waldy parked in Ash's slot. The garage was dark. The headlights glared against the concrete wall. Ash sat looking at the wall, he seemed blinded to the lights shining on his name.

"That's it for the night, Waldy," Ash said. "We'll do something, whatever we've got to do, tomorrow."

"Right, Ash."

Ash got out of the car and turned toward the elevator. But Waldy sat in the car, headlights glaring against the wall. Ash called back: "That's it for tonight, Waldy. Tomorrow. You can go home now." Wherever that is, thought Ash, whatever rock you live under, and went to the elevator. When the elevator carriage came, Ash looked back and saw that the car was quiet and dark and empty. He hadn't seen Waldy go but he was gone. As the elevator doors closed on Ash he smiled at himself for ever worrying about Waldy. He would survive the wreckage to come. Rats always did, didn't they?

Ash rode the elevator to the top floor, the graveyards for the fuckups and quitters and snitches and punks, the floor where they had sent him to sit out his suspension. He walked down the empty hall to his office. They didn't even turn on the lights up here on the graveyard floor. A silvery haze poured through a window at the far end of the hall, spreading across the floor: it was the only way Ash could see his way, his penlight was on the blink again. Ash stood at the door to his office and looked back down the hall. He suppressed a shudder. This place was worse than a graveyard. Nobody ever came up here, not even to die.

Ash turned the key and went into his office. He left the room dark. The dark and the isolation—they only made what he had to do easier. He went to the window and drew up the blinds. Evening light spread over the room. Enough to see what he had to do.

Ash went to his desk and unlocked the flat top drawer and pulled it back. His hand reached toward the file folders placed there, but stopped without touching them. He unlocked the deep bottom drawer and withdrew surgical gloves and put them on. Then he sat down and took up the two files—the obscene letters Sid Mehring had received in New York and the obscene letters from Sid Mehring to his ward in Miami. The ones Ash had, well, with a little help from his friends, composed with such skill.

Ash lifted the phone receiver and dialed a number. The number rang twenty times before Ash hung up. "You aren't ever there, are you, you little bitch? But tonight that's good." Ash smiled. "Not at the Room again, surely, Lex dear?" Ash opened the book. The light had dimmed so that he couldn't see the figures. He tried the penlight: still dead. He took a penny box of matches from his pocket, shook out a match, struck it and held it close to the book. He found the entry he was looking for:

THE ROOM—LEX

Ash dialed the number. In time a man's voice came on the line. Ash spoke into the receiver:

"You aren't home.

—Mehring's arrived. Right on schedule.

—No, I took him under my wing. Berger was at the airport.

—He didn't even try. He's waiting. You know how Mal likes to prolong things.

—Mehring? I left him at his hotel. We went to the Cut and the morgue. The usual tourist traps.

—Of course he suspects. Everyone *suspects*. It's knowing that counts.

—Have you found By yet? You better *not* have lost him, dear," Ash said sharply, but then he laughed. He felt brilliant, cold. His plan was still perfect, even if little By was out of the fold. Ash laughed again, like the sound of ice cracking.

"Lex, dear, By is stupid, but do you really think he's that stupid—to come back to the girl's apartment?

—I think you *like* watching her, Lex.

—Yes, of course. Of course. By will come to you. Or Daddy. The difference is the same.

—No. Berger let us go at the morgue. I don't know why but he's gone. He's really not out there.

—Ah yes, the letters," said Ash, lifting one of the documents from its file and looking at it. The room had grown too dark to read it. "I have both sets now. The Miami *and* the New York letters—Mehring to the girl and the girl to Mehring. They're perfect.

—Haven't I always told you it's the smart ones who are the easiest to trap?

—The plan is clean. I've got the gun with By's prints. I'll take it and the letters to By's place, then I'll call Mehring at his hotel—

—Exactly. Mehring is the key. He can't be left alive. And of course his death will take By and the girl with him. Mehring's death will even take Felix off our hands.

—*You* will have to take care of Anza, dear.

—Yes, Berger will be a problem. He's the only one I've ever been worried about, but with Mehring and By and the girl gone—

—That's true. Lex, you do still have your eye on the soapbox?

—Lex, I only want to know where it is to protect us. What if they move it? What if we have to kill them before we find out where it is? What, dear, if something should happen to you?

—Now, now—surely you can take a joke.

—How much longer will you be at the Room?

—My night shouldn't last long. An hour at By's apartment, to arrange things. I'll call Mehring at eight o'clock. It'll be over by nine. I don't want to go to the mansion before morning. Let Felix Racicot sleep his last night in peace.

—Midnight, then, at your place. You will be there, won't you?

—*Pas de problème*, Lex dear, *pas de problème*.

—Okay. Bye-bye."

Ash fitted the receiver back in the cradle. For a time he leaned back in the chair and watched the gray light in the window fade to black. He then reached into the deep drawer and brought out a pistol—a German automatic wrapped in plastic. He slipped the pistol in his pocket, took up the letter folders and went to the door of his office. He went into the hall and turned toward the elevator.

The car moved easily through the streets. Ash smiled as he drove. The tenements, the freaks, the grime, everything about the cop's life—coke, murder, betrayal—he was leaving it all behind. One more night of coke, murder and betrayal and he would be gone. Ash liked the poetry of it, the mathematical elegance. The very things he loathed, that were rotting his soul, tonight would set him free. He would steal and kill and sell drugs to the men he had taken them from and by morning he would be a good man again.

Ash touched the letter file on the seat beside him. In the beginning the letters had been such a stupid, childish idea. Lex or Felix—Ash couldn't remember whose idea the letters had been. Some sort of revenge against Mehring that Ash had never understood and never cared to. To incriminate some rich bastard in New York in a Florida drug burn—it was mad—but Ash had gone along with Lex and Felix and they had written the letters. But now Ash had the mad letters and he was twisting them to his own end. Making a rope that would hang Lex and little By as murderous blackmailers when the letters were found in Lex's apartment by Sid Mehring's dead body. As for Felix, Ash could always count on him. Felix would eliminate himself when his son went. And then Ash would be alone with the cocaine, with nothing left to do but stage his own death. Ash smiled. When he staged his own death he would do it right. When Ash died they would all believe he was really and truly dead.

Ash turned the unmarked car away from Byron Racicot's apartment, away from the girl's apartment and the Room across the street where Lex watched and waited, and went into the Grove, its twisted, crumbling streets lined with trees and vines and old wood-frame houses. When Ash saw the stucco apartment building on the corner, he stopped and parked. He turned off the headlights and watched the stucco building on the corner. The window of Lex's apartment was dark. Ash felt the pistol in his jacket and took up the letter file and got out of the car. He went to the trunk of the car and opened it. He slipped on the surgical gloves once again and took a typewriter case from the trunk, closed the lid and went across the street, toward the stucco building. He passed behind a parked red car, a cab. Ash noticed that the red cab was facing the stucco apartment, so that its occupant, if it had had one, might see Lex's window. But Ash thought nothing of the cab. Why the cab was parked watching the stucco building had nothing to do with Ash, it was no part of his plan, and he went on toward the stucco building.

Ash went through a courtyard entrance and up an open staircase to an open hall. The courtyard below was dark. The hall and stairs were dark, as if they were paneled with slate. A light came from an apartment down the way and Ash heard a TV in one of the apartments below. Somewhere a small dog barked. Ash went along the balcony hall to apartment 201. He took the penlight from his pocket and shook it. It was working again. He played the light on the door. A card with the name

LEX

was fitted in the plastic window below the bell. Ash slid a key in the lock, turned the knob and went into the dark apartment.

Ash left the apartment dark. He would not need to see to complete the night's plan. He could be blind and do what he had to do. He crossed the room to the desk, where he placed the typewriter case. The desk sat by the window looking down on the street. He could see the unmarked car and the red cab nearby. The street was dark and quiet. Ash felt for the venetian-blind cord, but it was gone. He reached up and worked the blinds down by hand, smoothing them flat, as if they were feathers or scales on a fish or a snake. He then turned away from the window. He sat at the desk, placing the file folder beside the typewriter case. He took the pistol from his pocket, stripped the plastic from it and put the pistol by the folder. He took up the phone on the desk and dialed a number. His voice purred into the receiver:

"Hotel Omni? Mr. Mehring's room, please.

—Thank you."

As Ash waited he listened to the sounds in the apartment. A water faucet dripping. A soft scurrying, then silence —a rat or a roach. These boys lived like pigs. The hotel operator came back on the line.

"Yes, I see. How long ago did he leave?

—Yes. And you have no idea when he'll return? This is very, very important. I must get in touch with Mr. Mehring right away.

—Yes. You might call it an emergency.

—My name? Donald Lexington.

—Yes, that's it. Please ask Mr. Mehring to meet me as soon as possible at 817 New London Street, Apartment 201.

—Perfect. Could you tell Mr. Mehring it concerns the letters.

—Yes. Tell him I know who wrote the letters.

—That's it. Thank you."

Ash put down the receiver. He sat trembling, his hands shaking. He held his fists between his knees. He leaned back in the chair, breathing deeply. He tried to smile, but his wonderful mask only trembled at the effort. He laughed. He could only talk to himself. "Ash, Ash, Ash, why let such a thing so upset you? Such a little thing. So it won't be Mehring who dies and Lex who hangs. So it will be Lex, he will die. And By will hang. Or the girl. Or Felix. What difference could it possibly make? Ash will walk in the end." And the cop leaned back and laughed, he was so afraid of what he had to do.

Ash turned to the typewriter he had placed on the desk and opened the case. He worked the penlight, shaking it, it was dead again. He flung the light across the room. He thought of the red car outside, facing the window of Lex's apartment. He reached forward and split open the blinds. The red car was still there: still empty. A laugh burst from Ash, a snarl of contempt he held back for his inferiors— Waldy or By or the silly girl—but now he was lashing himself for being so afraid. But it did not help. Nothing did. When he rolled paper into the machine he lurched at the whirr made by the mechanism. He waited, but his hands would not stop shaking. He could not type. Not in the dark. And the letter he would write, the final letter, the letter he thought he could write in his sleep, in the dark, Ash was so confused, so frightened he couldn't write it. He couldn't remember the obscenities of the other letters, he couldn't remember the awkward, childish style he had developed. He couldn't make up the filth, not any longer. He would have to copy the other letters. He would have to have light.

Ash sat trying to think. What was *wrong* with him? What was driving him to distraction over these silly things, the obscene letters, the dead penlight, the red cab, the dark? It wasn't By or Mehring or the girl. They could drop from the earth and he wouldn't bat an eye. Was it being back in Lex's apartment? No, it wasn't this place. Everything, almost everything, had happened at the Room. Lex? No, it wasn't Lex. Ash looked deep into himself and was pleased with what he saw. He felt nothing. Not for Lex, not for anyone. He would always have that. Ash smiled. This was the real Ash, cold and clean and controlled. Ash laughed at what was driving him mad tonight. The old Ash, now he understood it was the small things, the simple things, that drive men over the edge. It was the dripping water faucet. Nothing more. A dripping faucet, a squeaking board, a crooked frame, anything lose or unbalanced or out of place had always driven him crazy. In this act of murder and betrayal he had forgotten that a dripping water faucet could drive a man mad.

Ash rose from the desk and listened. The water dripping. Nothing else. Still, when he had come into the apartment there had been some other noise, a rustling, mice or roaches, maybe something larger. Ash took the German automatic from the desk, slid the receiver back and moved it forward with his hand. With the pistol raised, he went into the dark apartment, toward the ticking sound of falling water.

Ash left the dripping faucet till last. He went through the apartment room by room, seeing that it was empty, harmless, moving toward the bathroom, in the rear, where the tapping came from. Ash left the rooms and entered the hall. He went more slowly now, with greater care, in the hall. It was narrow and dark. And there was what Ash had seen in this hall, in other halls. It was where Lex liked—what word would describe it?—the halls were where Lex liked to play.

Ash stopped midway down the hall. Something came from the bathroom. An odor so strong it was a stench. An antiseptic chemical smell, like something being washed. Ash went forward toward the bathroom.

Ash stopped before the threshold. He pushed back the door. The room was shallow across, deep to his right. He pushed the door back till it struck the wall. He stepped into the room. To his left was the sink. There was a mirror and a medicine cabinet above the sink. Directly across from the door was the shower—a tub with a shower installed. The shower curtain was pulled closed around its aluminum ring. The dripping came from behind the curtain, from the tub or the shower. Ash turned to the deep end of the room, to the right, where it was dark. He could not see anything there.

Ash went to the short end of the room, to the left. He pulled back the medicine-cabinet door, seeing himself in the mirror before it swung back. Nothing. He turned and with his left hand reached toward the shower curtain. He took the plastic and pulled it hard. The curtain rings shrieked against the metal hanging rod. Breath hissed from Ash's throat. There, in the tub, was a mound of white powder. The cocaine. The fools had put ten million dollars in the bathtub! But even as Ash went to his knees, even as he drove his fingers deep into the white powder, he knew something was wrong. The greasy feel of the powder, the sharp chemical stench, the movement, some blur of light at the far, dark end of the room—Ash knew something there was wrong.

Ash came to his feet. The gun was gone. He had dropped it in the soap powder, but he could not look for it. He could not take his eyes off the blur at the dark end of the room. A picture, a photograph, something with a face, shined dully at the end of the room. Ash went toward it.

Ash was but a few feet from the end of the room when he saw himself in the frame. The white blur had been his own face in a mirror. Ash turned and looked back where he had been. There at the distant end of the room he saw a tiny shrunken head. Blurred, white, contorted, it hung from the wall above the sink. Ash knew it was only his face in another mirror, the mirror on the medicine cabinet, but he cried out at the decapitated head hanging there. He ran for the door. He slipped on something on the floor. He fell. He was on the floor, on his hands and knees. He looked up at the shrunken head. It was gone. Ash fought to control himself. To beat back his panic. Of course his reflection would be gone, with him on the floor. But then Ash saw that the medicine-cabinet door was canted open. What he had seen in the mirror hadn't been his face at all. It had been a face reflected from somewhere else. From the hall. Ash turned toward the door to the hall. The face came through the door—white, enormous—moving for him, moving faster than he had ever seen anything move before. Ash did not have time to cry out again.

The man moved through the apartment, as quiet as he had gone before. He left the bathroom and went along the hall. He crossed the main room to the desk where the cop had sat, where the cop had spoken on the phone, where he had cursed the typewriter and the dark. The man saw the letter file open on the desk. A small address book lay on the letters. The man struck the lighter he had taken from the cab and held the flame over the address book. He read through the book till he came to the entry:

THE ROOM—LEX

The man took up the phone and dialed the number. After a time a man's voice came on the line. The voice was soft and taunting, amused.

"Yes?"

The man who had called said nothing.

The voice came again, sharper: "Ash?"

The man said, "Lex?"

"Who is this? By, is this you, you little cunt?"

"Lex, where are you?"

There was silence now, then the voice again, tight, high: "Who is this?"

The man broke the connection. He turned back to the small address book. He went through the book to the S section. There he found the name Jamie Simmons and an address for the girl. The man rose. He saw the file folder on the desk. He opened it and snapped the lighter. He glanced through the first letter in the file, and the second. Then he began to read.

TWELVE

THE boy took the rubber rope and twisted it around his biceps and pumped up his arm till the vein inside his elbow showed blue and gnarled through the skin. The girl knew it was a show, she knew how much he hated and feared the needle, she knew he would shoot the muscle, that he could barely do that, he so feared the pain of the needle. The girl knew all this, that he did these things for another man, but she didn't care. She knew everything about the boy, *everything*, and she still loved him. She was sick with fear that the boy might leave her, that she might do something wrong, that she might not be with the boy every minute of her life, for the rest of her life. That was her love for the boy, her sickness.

The boy saw the girl watching him as he took the needle to his arm. He saw the look on her face, the secret glance of understanding and devotion, and he hated her for it. He hated her for watching him, for knowing his fear, knowing everything about him. He hated her, more than he had ever hated anything, for loving him.

The boy took the needle to his arm but he could not take it farther. He could not break the skin. He held the needle steady, close to the skin, and turned to the girl. Now that he faced her she was not watching him. The boy hated that most, her secret watching, her eyes turned away now that he had turned to her.

"What are you looking at?" said the boy.

"Nothing," said the girl. Her eyes were turned down. She raised her face to the boy, but still her eyes were cast down to the floor.

"You were watching me."

"No. No," said the girl. "I wasn't."

"You were," said the boy and held the needle toward her. "You want it, don't you?"

The girl felt herself go small inside, she shrank from where the boy was leading her. "No. No, I don't want it. I wasn't watching you."

"You were. You want it." The boy was standing now, holding the needle. "Say you want it. Tell me where you want it. Tell me how you want it."

The girl shook her head. Now was the time for her to say what the boy wanted, how he wanted it, but she could not. She could not give him everything he wanted, she could not say she wanted it, not anymore. She had to have something for herself. "I don't want it. I only want you." The boy watched the girl. He made no sound but to breathe as his fury grew. The girl did not have to raise her eyes to see his face—the contortions of his rage. She sat waiting for the blow. His voice came in a hiss, the words dead, unconnected things, without meaning:

"Tell me you want it!"

The girl had begun to weep. She could say nothing but "No. No. No."

The pain struck the girl's shoulder suddenly, sharp, like the sting of a bee. She saw the boy's face before she saw what had caused the pain. His rage had gone. His face had gone white. His mouth had broken open. His eyes were dull, glazed with fear and cowardice.

The girl followed the boy's gaze to her shoulder. There, at the point of the sting, the hypodermic syringe jutted from her shoulder. She cried out and twisted away from the needle, as if it were some bloodsucking thing that had fastened to her flesh. She could not bring herself to touch the needle to wrench it from her muscle. The girl came off the bed where she had been and crawled away from the thing the boy had thrown into her. She crawled back till she reached a wall and could go no farther.

The boy came to her gently. He held her firmly against the wall and took the syringe and pulled it from her shoulder. When the sting was gone the girl curled up on the floor and wept. The boy took the needle away and returned and took up the girl and lifted her onto the bed. There he laid her out and brought something to press against her shoulder, though the needle had left nothing but numbness and a spot of blood. The boy sat on the floor by the bed and murmured to the girl, stroking her. The boy spoke of the things he always spoke of when he was gentle with the girl—he spoke of the past and of their memories, he spoke of their dreams. It was while listening to the boy whisper this litany that the girl, finally, after two wakeful nights, fell asleep.

When the girl woke she did not know where she was. She lay on a bed, the room was dark, she was alone. She did not rise up in panic as she might have done. She lay soothed by the dark. The empty room brought her peace. It was only when the girl remembered where she was and that she had not always been alone, it was only when she remembered what they had done that she became afraid.

The girl sat up. Now the dark and the loneliness were hell. She wanted to scream, to cry out the boy's name. She wanted this more than she wanted life, but she did not speak. She waited there in the dark, praying for some sign of the boy, that he had not left her. When she heard the sound beyond one of the doors—water rushing in a sink—she lay back on the bed, limp, tears falling across her face. The boy had not left her. Not yet.

The door opened and the boy came into the room. He looked at the girl on the bed and saw that she had not changed her attitude of sleep. He went to the other bed, only a few feet from the girl. He sat on the bed and breathed deeply, twice, a third time, a fourth, then he lay out on the bed. The girl did not turn her head to look at the boy, but she knew his eyes were closed, his face soft and unformed as it always was before sleep, when he had taken a pill. The girl lay in the dark waiting for the sound of the boy sleeping. But the girl could not wait for the boy to sleep, not tonight. She would take his rage, anything but waiting for the boy to sleep and to wake. She spoke his name:

"By?"

There was nothing. The girl knew the boy was awake. He was pretending to sleep.

"By?" she said again.

There was a sound. The boy turned on the bed. His voice came heavy, as if he were waking or drugged.

"What?"

"Are you asleep?"

"Not now."

97

The girl waited. "Are you okay?"

A contemptuous laugh came from the boy. "Yeah. I'm okay."

The girl waited. "By?"

"I'm By."

"What are we going to do?"

There was a silence, then the boy spoke. His voice was cool, clear. "We've got to check the locker. One of us has to go out."

The girl heard the words as a sentence of death passed on her. She pulled herself up. "Why?"

"Why, baby? Twenty-four hours of why."

"Twenty-four hours?"

"Baby, twenty-four hours—we have to put our quarters in the locker every twenty-four hours or they'll come and take our suds away."

The girl waited. "Let's let them, By."

The boy spoke slowly. "Let them, baby?"

"Let's let them take it away."

The boy laughed softly. He spoke as he had spoken of their dreams. "No, baby, we can't let them take our suds away. We have to put the quarters in the slot, baby."

"By, I don't want to be away from you. Please."

The boy turned on his side. The girl could see his face, the way she remembered it, dim and young and beautiful. "You've got to go out, baby. For me," the boy said. "I can't go out. You understand that. Anza, the Colombians, they're crawling the town looking for me. Do you know what they'll do to me if they find me? Do you know?"

The boy's voice had risen. The girl would do anything, she would leave him, she would give him away, if only he would be like her dreams. "I'll go," she said. "I'll go. They won't recognize me. They don't know me," she said. "Do you have the key?"

"The key?"

"The locker key," the girl said. "You have it. You said you had to keep it with you."

The boy rose from the bed and went to the bureau across the room. He reached behind the bureau, where he had hidden the key. The boy turned and came toward the girl with the key held in the palm of his hand. He displayed the key before the girl, and she took it. The girl looked on the key as a deformed thing, heavy in her small hand, a square knob of plastic from which jutted a small jagged sheath of steel. They would kill her for this key, any number of them, they would kill the girl and kill her easily for the key and the ten million dollars' worth of cocaine they had stolen. But that was not the death the girl saw in her hand. She saw the key taking away more than her life. The key would take her away from the boy and when she returned she knew the boy would be gone. The key opened nothing. It closed everything.

The boy kissed the girl, tenderly, almost as if he wanted to, and she rose and went out the door.

By lay on his side on the bed facing the wall. He waited five minutes, ten, longer, till he was sure the girl was gone. Then he rolled on his back and looked toward the door and smiled. He rose and went to the door and listened. He could hear nothing but the sound of the street outside the door. He locked the door and returned to the bed. He sat on the bed and switched on the lamp on the small table between the beds. He reached for the telephone on the table. Now the boy's face was set, anxious. He took up the phone. He dialed the number of the Room in the building across from the girl's apartment, the number Ash had called, the number the man who had killed Ash had found in the cop's book.

99

The same voice the man had heard came over the line, but now the voice was sharp, angry. By did not understand.

"It's me.

—No. No! It wasn't—I swear, Lex, it wasn't me. Why would I—

—Ash? Why would he call the Room—

—I know, I *know* I don't have that right.

—Lex, why are you *doing* this to me? What are you doing?

—I don't know. I'm sorry. I said I'm sorry, you fuck!

—No, please don't. *Please*! Lex. I'm just nervous. Nerves nerves nerves. *I'm* the one they're after—remember?

—Gone. Finally. She's been on me like skin.

—No. She's gone to the station.

—No, I'll be gone when she gets back. It's as good a way as any to get rid of her.

—No, she's okay. She won't talk.

—I know she won't. I *know* her. I *know* she won't.

—No, Lex, no. Leave her alone! *Don't*!

—Lex, please, she's as good as dead anyway. She can't tell them anything, even if she wanted to. She doesn't know anything.

—No. I haven't called him yet.

—Lex, let's take the box and go. New York, anywhere.

—Lex, I can't deal with Daddy. I just can't. He's so—I don't know what.

—No, not innocent.

—Yes. I want you too.

—Yes. Everything. All of it. I'm ready now. What difference could it make now?

—All right. I'll call when I have the money.

—No. It's all arranged. I've talked to Jimmy.

—Yes. Okay.

—I love you," said the boy and sat listening to the

hazy sound of the disconnected line. At length he placed the receiver in its cradle. Now that he had made the first call, he would make the second. What else could he do? There was no other place for him to turn but home. He wiped his face. His hands felt as if they were covered with blood, his sweat tacky, clinging to his fingers. He took up the phone and dialed another number. A man's voice came on the line. The boy said:

"Jimmy. It's By. May I speak to my father, please?"

By waited a time. There came the sound of another phone on the line being lifted.

"Daddy, it's Byron. Daddy, can I talk to you?

—I'm in trouble, Daddy. Bad trouble. *Real* trouble.

—I want to come home. Can I come home?

—Now.

—Daddy, thank you. Thank you, Daddy. Thank you. Thank you.

—Now. I'm coming now.

—I love you, Daddy, I love you," said the boy and broke off the connection before the man on the line could make a reply.

Jamie walked away from the motel quickly, without knowing where she was going, just moving, going away from the boy and the squalid room. She would walk and walk and walk and never again see the boy and his twisted love or the millions that was theirs now or the brutal men they had stolen from. But after a few minutes the girl's will to flee collapsed and she stopped. Jamie stood on some night-thrashed street and was ill, vomiting without shame before the stream of sleek cars and gawking tourists and crowds of bums and winos who jeered at her and cried out and waved their bottles in derision. Jamie cleaned her face and mouth and moved away from where she had felt finally, at last, after years of descending day by day, moment by moment, that she had reached the pit of hell that had been her love for the boy. There was no deeper, more terrible place her love could draw her, she thought, than this filthy corner with the winos jeering, the car horns honking, the little tourists, children or small savage people leaning their heads out the windows, pointing at the miserable, sick girl, jabbing their fingers at her as if they might take out her eyes.

As Jamie walked she remembered the street she was on. An avenue, wide, double lanes, a string of palms marking the center—the street ran by the motel and went on, in the direction she was going, toward downtown and the bus station, to the locker where By had hidden the cocaine. Jamie gripped the locker key in her pocket and went along the street, walking quickly, her head down, seeing nothing as she went and not being seen.

The girl came to the bus station. She pushed through a glass door and went past a wall of magazine racks and came into a large hall that was filled with people yet rang hollow and empty, that was brightly lit but whose walls and floors and ceiling were dark as night. The people here had come to flee those they hated, to be torn from those they loved, but there were no such passions in the hall. Only numbness, stupor, exhaustion. Drifters with all they owned or would ever own in shopping bags, rolled in blankets, tied in bandannas; broken families, mothers with sick, failing children, fathers leaving them behind, off to some other bus station, to be greeted there by loneliness and despair; hookers so old and deformed nobody wanted them, not for a dollar, not for a dime; hustlers whose nerves were gone, whose tricks were stale; their marks laughed at them and took their money; the runaways, boys, girls, some who had come here to go home, some having fled home, the despair of coming the same as the despair of going; young soldiers ending leave, off to some outpost of an empire they didn't even know existed; then everywhere the winos, bums, freaks, with their gutted faces, angry, empty eyes, their only decoration scab, tattoo and scar. Jamie passed unnoticed through the bus station. Still wearing the drowned woman's shirt, the reek of vomit about her, despairing, the girl was one of them.

Jamie went through the bus station, toward the back, where the lockers were. For a time she stood looking at the wall of small tan doors with squat plastic keys projecting from their frames. She took the key from her pocket and went down the bank of lockers till she found the number on the key. She placed the key before the lock, and then she froze. Her sight went dim. She dropped her hand. She began shaking, struck by a furious desperation. Money, no money, she didn't have the two quarters to relock the locker. Had she put the key in the lock she would have had ten million dollars in a soap box and no place to hide it. She turned away from the locker and went into the hall.

Now Jamie saw they were watching her as she moved through the hall. A black man wearing sunglasses came toward her. She turned away. A white woman with piled white hair wearing white-rimmed glasses and a white cowgirl jacket stood in her path. The black man stroked her back as she went toward the glistening white woman. The white woman pushed her away. Jamie went in another direction, the black man walking beside her, his face lowered to her, whispering loathsome things, the white woman calling out threats and insults. Jamie lowered her head. She went through the hall without hope.

Jamie saw the dark trousers and dark shoes and the briefcase the man carried, she saw his soft ordinary face, and she went toward him. She stopped in front of the man.

She blocked his way. She knew something was wrong, she could hear the man breathing as she spoke.

"Can you loan me some money? Please. Two quarters. Anything."

"Money?" came the reply. "How much do you want?"

Jamie raised her eyes. The man's mouth was a hole in his face, stretching, contracting, filled with something wet and rotten. His eyes were black, empty holes. "Two quarters. Fifty cents. I need it for a locker. *Please*."

The voice squirted. "What do you need a locker for?" He raised his briefcase. "I've got it all in here. Everything we'll need."

"No, no, no," cried the girl and turned away, pleading for someone, anyone, to understand and to help.

The man followed behind, working his tongue near her ear. The briefcase was held against her: she could feel something squirming, something alive, in it. "Soon you'll be in here too. And I won't let you out either."

Jamie turned and in a fury flung aside the briefcase and went toward the man. "Goddamn you, leave me alone! Leave me alone! All of you!" And the man with the soiled mouth and burnt eyes stepped back, he faded in the crowd, again an ordinary man hurrying home from work.

Jamie turned to the others now that her anger had given her strength, but they were gone. They were still there, all around her, but they no longer cared. The black pimp, the cracker cowgirl, they didn't look at her anymore. They didn't even know she was there.

Jamie began to think as she grew stronger. She would return to the locker. She would take the box and return to the motel room. By would be there, she knew he would, he loved her. She would tell him, she would explain, the locker was too dangerous, it was a silly idea anyway, some strange notion of Lex's. They, she and By, they would take the cocaine, just the two of them, and they would run. And the other silly ideas, that her lover, the love of her life, would abandon her, would be gone and this nightmare would be over.

Jamie returned to the lockers. She went directly to the locker and inserted the key and turned it and opened the door. The girl staggered. She had to grasp the locker door to keep from falling, her legs had gone from under her. She raised her head. The locker was empty. She put her arm in the locker and reached into the back. There was nothing there. The box of soap was gone. Jamie turned away. *The cocaine was gone.* She started to walk away, somewhere, into the night, but she stopped. She laughed. How stupid, how silly she was. The box wasn't gone, she merely had opened the wrong locker. The box was there, in another locker. She wasn't thinking. She was such a fool.

Jamie went back to the locker. She felt strong again. The key had a number on it, the right number. She would take the key and find the right number and the right locker and there—there the box would be and everything would be all right. She grasped the key and pulled, but it wouldn't come loose. The key was stuck. She grasped the knob and pulled as hard as she could. She began to cry that everything was so wrong—the wrong locker, the stuck key, the dead woman's shirt, it had no change, no quarters in it—and she cried out her fury till she became calm again and began to think again. The key was not stuck. It was not the wrong locker. The numbers matched. There was nothing wrong, nothing except that ten million dollars' worth of cocaine was gone.

Jamie went back into the hall. There, high on the wall, hung a large clock. Twenty-four hours. They removed a locker's contents after twenty-four hours, that was what By had said. Jamie watched the clock. Eight o'clock. It was dark now. When had By put the case in the locker? Last night sometime. She wasn't sure. It seemed like it had been late, later than eight o'clock. But she couldn't remember. Maybe it had been earlier. Twenty-four hours had passed. They had come and taken the case away, just because they had broken their stupid, stupid rule. Twenty-four hours and her entire life was over. Jamie turned away from the clock. She felt numb as death.

She saw the man watching her as soon as she started across the hall toward the door. He wasn't like the others who had watched her. They had been part of her fear and panic. This man was different, not a bum or a pimp or a freak. He was really watching her, *her*, Jamie Simmons. He knew who she was. Even now, as she changed directions and went away from him, he came after her. A fat-faced little man wearing thick-rimmed glasses that weighed heavily on his sweaty nub nose, he came toward Jamie, holding a newspaper in his hand, open, displaying it, like a newsboy.

"Hey! Hey you!" he called out and went across her path, bumping his little paunch into Jamie.

Jamie had had enough. "Buzz off, jerk," she said and made a fist and bounced it under the little man's chin, the chunk one would make to tease a baby, but much harder. The little man's glasses popped off his face. He waved the paper about, feeling his face for his missing specs.

"Wanted! Wanted! Wanted!" he squealed.

Then Jamie saw the paper and herself, a picture of herself half a foot high spread over the front page and beneath her picture in black bold type:

**WANTED FOR
QUESTIONING**

Jamie pushed away from the fat, squealing man and ran toward the main exit, but there the newspaper racks barred her way, a fanned tier of papers, her face repeated like shingles, stacked everywhere, and the words,

WANTED FOR
WANTED FOR
WANTED FOR

Jamie turned back to the hall and she ran and ran till she found a way out and then she ran into the night.

The girl came to the avenue that led back to the motel. The palms stood in line down the avenue center, their trunks curved, fronds drooping, like creatures saddened by her plight, listening powerlessly to her prayers that the boy had not gone. The girl came to the motel and stood at the end of the walk. The doors stretched out in line, each like the others, the rooms behind them identical, everything about them the same. The girl went along the doors searching for the boy. She tried every door. They were locked. All of them. She knocked on every door. Nothing. Door after door, the room was always empty. The boy was always gone.

The girl turned away from the motel. She walked. She did not think or look where she was going. Then she began to see where she was. She began to recognize streets and buildings and signs. And with seeing where she was, where she was going, the girl began to think, about the boy and why he was gone and where. And by thinking the girl began to have hope and hope brought back memories and all these things brought her an understanding of why the boy was gone. And with these false thoughts and false memories and

107

false hopes and false understanding came the falsest friend of all. The girl became happy.

Jamie went quickly toward the apartment where she had once lived. Why wouldn't By be there? It was where they had begun. Where they had been happy and in love. Before they had become something else. Home, that was what she had called it. And the boy too, it had been his home. Away from his father and Lex and the others. They had been children when they lived there, the girl knew that, children playing adults, but still, wouldn't the boy go back there too? Wouldn't he yearn for those times? The girl knew he would, as surely as she had ever known anything. The words rang in her mind. The boy had gone home.

Now that the girl had neared her old apartment she went more slowly. Her fear had returned. She could not open another empty thing. The locker, the motel room, if the boy was not here, at the old apartment, she knew she would be completely mad. Now that the girl's fear had returned she looked around. She had walked more quickly than she knew. She was home. Her old apartment would be there, above her. She only had to look up. She only had to open her eyes.

The girl cried out when she saw the figure standing in the window of her old apartment. She wept, she laughed. The boy was there, as she knew he would be, and here she was standing in the middle of the street, cars flying past her on all sides. What a fool she was. Now that everything was all right again, that her prayers had been answered, that she and the boy would be together again, now would be the time for a fool to stand in the traffic in the middle of the street.

The girl ran from the traffic, between two parked cars, onto the sidewalk. She went into the apartment lobby. People were milling about there, waiting for the elevator, their eyes lifted to the arrow that marked the car's descent. Fourth, third, the second floor—as the car reached the ground floor the crowd was split apart by a man trying to break to its head, to get to the elevator first. Jamie fought against the crowd. She could not be left behind. The people cursed the man who fought through them and they cursed Jamie but she got onto the elevator and then got out again. She went down the hall. She came to the door of her old apartment. It was open. She called out the boy's name. Nothing. She went in. Every light in the apartment was on.

"By. By," she said and went into each room. He wasn't there. He had been there, at the window, only moments ago, but now he was gone.

The girl went through the apartment again. She tore open every door, every cupboard, she looked everywhere. Her search sent her into a frenzy. She looked in the maddest places, places so small the boy could never have hidden there. But she tore into these places all the same, calling for him.

Jamie came to the window, where she had seen the figure standing. She looked down to the street. She could see nothing there. Then something drew her to the building across the way. Another tall apartment building facing hers like a mirror. A man was there, standing in a lighted window, looking out toward her, gesturing toward her. Now she saw there were two men in the room. There was somebody else standing behind the first man, back, away from the window. The second man came forward—the man at the window didn't know he was there. Now Jamie saw the second man, his face. The second man was Lex. Jamie tried to cry out, to warn the man at the window, but Lex raised something in his hand and he brought it forward and down and the girl closed her eyes and screamed.

When the girl looked again they were gone. The room

across the way was dark. It was as if they had never been there, as if it all had happened in her mind. She left the apartment, exhausted, numb, understanding nothing. The elevator car was gone. She walked down the stairs. She went into the street without looking. A car braked and swerved around her.

The girl no longer cared. If the man at the window had been By he was dead. Lex had killed him. If it hadn't been By, then By was gone. The girl didn't know which and didn't care. She went into the building across the way. She took the elevator and got off. She had no idea which floor the two men had been on. She went along the corridor. There in a dark corner by the stairwell crouched an old man. The old man raised his finger and croaked, "Up there."

The girl went up the stairs. She went along the corridor. She found the door to the room open. She looked in. A body lay across the room, by the open window. Jamie went toward the body. She grasped the man's shoulder and turned him. It wasn't By. The girl pushed the man's shoulder and he went back to the way he had been. The girl knew the man, she remembered his face. He wasn't By, but he was someone she had once loved as she loved the boy, only the girl could not remember when or where she had loved the man Lex had killed.

The girl left the apartment and walked. She went through the city. She walked through it all—the winos, the bums, the hustlers, the hawkers, the tourists, the freaks—and she saw nothing. She walked and walked and in time came to a dark, deserted square. A park, a place where people came during the day and sat on the benches and chatted and ate lunch and watched the tourists and freaks promenade. But now the plaza was empty, dark. There was nothing here now but rapists and muggers. The girl went into the park and found a bench. Rapists and muggers, the girl thought—

110

after tonight, bring them on. The girl smiled. Maybe there was hope for her yet. What had her brother said—something about joking, something, she couldn't remember, if you could laugh there was hope.

The girl thought of her brother. She hadn't thought of him, not like this, not *remembering* him, for years. Not since she had come to hate him. Since the boy and Lex had taught her to hate him. Why had she hated him? He was in a war somewere. He was killing people who didn't need to be killed. She remembered that and then the way he really was and she began to weep. Her sorrow was not like before, her weeping did not tear her apart. It was healing.

A plane came low from behind one of the tall buildings that surrounded the square, huge, spectral, silent till it came over her. The ground around the girl trembled as the plane passed overhead, but it was gone quickly and the park was quiet again. The girl looked at the building the plane had come over. On the building top a large neon sign was laid over a billboard. There was a picture of a plane on the billboard, like the plane that had flown over the park. The neon glowed in the night. The words said:

Fly New York

The girl thought of New York, as she had thought of her brother. She remembered the man who lived there, the man who had been her brother's friend in the war, who had become her guardian when her brother was killed. She remembered her love of this man she had never seen and the hatred they had taught her for him. He had said something, she couldn't remember the words, some forgiveness for the terrible things they had written him. Now the girl remembered. If she ever needed him, if she was ever in trouble, she was to call. Those were the words. He was her guardian. Call.

The girl grew cold. She remembered the face of the man Lex had killed. It was the face of her guardian, her brother's friend, Captain Mehring. Jamie rose, numb. The man who could save her wasn't alive in New York. He was here in Miami and he was dead. Sid Mehring was the man Lex had killed in the room across the way. Still, Jamie went across the park toward the phone booth. There was nothing left for her to do but call.

Jamie went into the booth. She closed the door after her and the light came on. She lifted the receiver. The line was dead. But the girl laughed and her panic went away. A pay phone; the line would be dead till she put a coin in the slot. She felt in her pockets. Then she remembered the bus station and the locker. She remembered the clothes she was wearing and the woman she had taken them from. The girl leaned her face against the phone and cried out, "Money, my dear God, I have no money!"

The girl turned her face. There was something near. A tiny bin. The coin return. She reached her hand to the bin and pulled it open. She slid her finger into the curved drawer. There she felt a dime, a treasure left for the girl by a hurried caller. She took out the coin and made the call.

THIRTEEN

T HE Room was dark. The only light was that which came through the windows. A table and two chairs were placed before the windows. A phone sat on the table. Mattresses were put all about the floor. There were only narrow corridors between them on which to walk. Lex stood before the table looking out the window. He held a pair of binoculars in his left hand. He raised them to his eyes from time to time. Shadows fell across Lex's face, obscuring it. Nothing could be seen but his mouth, which was wide, the lips paper-thin, delicate, drawn like statuary. The flesh of the lips and the flesh of Lex's face were a common cold white.

Lex reached out and took the blind cord and lowered the blinds halfway, so that the upper windows were covered. He sat at the table. Watching the building was not his primary concern now. Now that Ash had called the Room,

113

and there had been the silent caller, the man who had only said Lex's name, now that the breather and Ash and finally the little fool By had called, Lex took up the phone. Now he would finish them all. He dialed the operator and gave her the number of a car phone. He hung up the phone and waited. In a few moments the phone rang and Lex picked up the receiver. His voice was concerned, sincere:

"Mr. Anza? I spoke to one of your associates earlier.

—That's right. My name is not important, Mr. Anza. Let's say I am a friend.

—Yes. A complete guaranteed return. Not one gram blown.

—No, this is not a joke, Mr. Anza. This is real. The Cessna serial number was DH498665. The island was Cay Yerba. The flight plan was filed in San Juan—

—Yes. That's right.

—I was in charge of ground operations. I prepared the strip, I constructed the decoy plane and set the camouflage for the mule. I wired the decoy with dynamite and diesel and when the mule touched down, I set off the explosion.

—It was rather elegant, wasn't it? But now, you see, I've seen the error of my ways. I didn't care for the drugs or the money, only to see if I could do it. A test of my intelligence against yours, you might say.

—Yes, I'm aware of the risk. But what harm has been done, Mr. Anza, if your product is returned?

—Yes, there is another reason that I want to make restitution—other than living a little longer. The Racicots kept me entirely in the dark concerning the upper reaches of the operation. I had no idea who we were ripping off. I had no idea of the size of the shipment or the importance of the dealer.

—Yes. Byron Racicot and his father. Felix Racicot.

—The girl is of little importance. A stooge for father and son.

—Yes. The pilots. Swede—

—Yes, and Mike too. He was witting as well, I'm afraid.

—And there was a third party—a man I've never met, but who had the connection to deal the product.

—Sergeant James Ashburn of the Miami police force. Narcotics, I believe.

—No. There were no others. Oh, I'm sure that Felix Racicot, a man of his wealth and influence, must have had associates—

—Yes, there was talk of a man from New York. Mehring. . . .

—I'm well aware of that, Mr. Anza. No one can hide forever. I'm only trying to buy some time. Perhaps when you do find me, you will be able to forgive.

—Thank you.

—No, no—I must be in charge of that. I'll deliver the package to you tonight—both the product and Byron Racicot. Shall we say the Yacht Harbor?

—No, I don't know how long it will take, but tonight. Very soon.

—And goodnight to you, sir," said Lex and put down the phone.

The last part of the call had been hurried. As Lex had been speaking he had seen a red cab pull up in front of the apartment building across the street, the building he had been watching. A short, athletic man with a hard face and sandy hair had gotten out of the cab, paid the driver and walked into the building across the way.

Lex stood and pulled the blind up as far as it would go. He took up the binoculars. Because of the sharp perspec-

tive—the Room where Lex watched was on the sixth floor—
Lex lost sight of the sandy-haired man after he went a few
feet into the lobby. But Lex knew the man had gone to the
elevator, that he had pressed the call button and was waiting
for the elevator to descend to the ground floor.

Lex raised the binoculars to the floor directly across
from the Room. Lex could see everything on that floor, the
hall and the elevator and into every major room in the
apartment of Jamie Simmons. He lowered the binoculars.
He had no need for them. He knew what he was going to
see. The stage was set.

When Sid Mehring had left his hotel he had hailed a
cab and given the driver the last address he had for Jamie
Simmons. The cab had stopped before the number and Sid
Mehring paid the driver and asked him to wait. Sid went
into the building and rode the elevator to the fifth floor, got
out and went down the corridor. Sid stopped before the
door of Jamie's apartment. He turned the knob. The door
came open and Sid stepped into the apartment. Every light
in the apartment was on.

Sid went through the apartment quickly. There was no
one there. He went to the window and looked down to the
street. The red cab was parked where Sid had left it. There
was nothing else. No sign of a police stakeout. Sid saw a
limousine stopped several yards behind the cab, but he
thought nothing of it. Sid looked at the building across the
way. The police might be watching from there, but he saw
nothing and turned back to the girl's apartment.

The apartment was bare. Little food in the kitchen, no
clothes in the closets, nothing in the bathroom, the desk
drawers were empty, no letters, address books, no bills or
notes or receipts or any sign of the girl. The phone was

dead. Two magazines lay on the coffee table. Both were dated over a year ago. The apartment had not been lived in for months. Sid Mehring turned to the object that had caught his eye the moment he had come into the apartment.

Someone had set up the two photographs like a shrine. One photograph was of Jamie Simmons's dead brother, the other of Sid Mehring. In both photographs the men were in uniform, Sergeant Simmons's a formal portrait, that of Sid a snapshot that he had sent the girl and that she had had enlarged and framed. Between the two photographs stood a small American flag. On a shelf beneath the photographs Sid found a Special Forces yearbook. Inside the yearbook was the signature of Roger Simmons. This sarcastic temple brought an anger to Sid Mehring that he had not known for years, a will to destroy that he had thought was dead. The person who had set these photographs here in this barren apartment was, he knew, the person, one of them anyway, who had written the obscene letters to and from him. And now this person, this freak who had lured Sid Mehring into a duel he did not understand, to battle an enemy he had never seen, now Sid Mehring knew he was near. He was here, in the room with him. Now.

Sid turned from the photographs. He listened. There was nothing there. He had searched every corner of the apartment. He had torn open every possible hiding place, and still Sid could feel him. Sid went to the open windows and looked out at the tropical evening. It had been dark for an hour, at least, and still there was a glow in the sky behind the building across the way. Sid looked into the windows of the apartment across the way. He saw nothing there. He looked down to the street. Traffic, pedestrians. The red cab was still there; perhaps it had moved a few feet backward. Sid could see the driver behind the wheel now. The man was leaning forward, his face pressed close to the windshield, looking up, not at Sid or the building he was in, but at the building across the street. Sid saw the driver's face. Before the cab had been dark and the driver had not looked at Sid. But now Sid saw the man and even at this distance, with the distortions of the curved windshield, a memory came to Sid. He had known that face in the past. Sid looked down again. The driver's face was gone. Then Sid saw a girl standing near the limousine, in the middle of the street. The girl was looking up, as the cab driver had. Sid thought about the girl, how lost and young she looked, she looked no more than twelve, wearing a baggy old shirt, standing in the middle of the street. Sid could not see the girl's face and he did not think that she might be Jamie Simmons. Sid turned away from the window. As he did he looked at the building across the way and he saw the man standing there watching him.

Sid did not know how he had not seen the man before. The light in the room across the way was on now, but still— he should have seen the freak in the dark. The man stood framed in the window, the light backing him so that Sid could not see his face, only that he was young and that he was mocking him. Sid saw the room behind the man, the bare walls, the ceiling. He saw the corner of a desk and the telephone and he saw the binoculars the man held. The man's hand moved down his body and then the man reached out to Sid, beckoning for him to come to him.

Sid leaped away from the window. He went through the door and ran down the hall. The elevator car was gone. Sid went down the stairs, three, four at a time. He came out into the lobby. The way was blocked by people waiting for the elevator. Sid slammed through the people in the lobby and came out on the street. Sid ran across the street and into the building across the way. The elevator car was gone from the ground floor, and Sid went up the stairs.

118

He did not know what story the man had been on, he had forgotten to think. He came out on a floor. He went along the hall. The room the man had been in—it was three, four from the end—he couldn't remember. He knocked on a door. Nothing. He tried the knob. Locked. He went to the next door. There was a sound within. Someone moving toward the door. Sid flattened himself against the wall. There was the sound of a bolt working. The door cracked open. Sid went hard against the door. The man who had opened the door went back. Sid came into the room. He took the man by the throat and drove him across the room, against the wall. Sid saw the man's face next to his. The brown, wrinkled skin, the watery eyes, the stinking breath, the choked words:

"I didn't do it."

Sid released the pumping throat and went to the window. He saw Jamie Simmons's apartment across the way. He had come a floor too low. The freak was on the floor above.

Sid went to the door. The old man was still pinned against the wall, like a dried specimen tacked to a board.

"You're not who I'm looking for," Sid said.

"Glad to hear it," the old man said.

Sid went up the stairs, moving slowly. At the top he waited, then went into the hall quickly, pressing against the wall. Nothing in the hall. Sid saw the open door, halfway down the hall, on the left. He went toward it. He paused outside the door, then went into the room quickly. He crouched in the room, a few feet from the door, and waited. He heard nothing. The room was dark now. He could see mattresses placed about on the floor and the table and the phone before the open window. Sid could feel it now, the easing off—the freak was gone. He had had his look and had run.

Sid went to the window. He saw Jamie Simmons's apartment as the freak had seen it—the windows open, curtains drawn, every room lit as if it were a stage. Sid saw the girl in the apartment across the way as the freak had seen him. It was the girl he had seen on the street below, the lost girl in soiled, baggy shirt. The girl was searching through the apartment as Sid had. Frantic, desperate. She flung back doors, opened closets, overturned furniture, looking for something or someone who wasn't there. The girl finished her search and came to the window. She looked across toward Sid. Sid knew who she was. He saw that the lost girl who had been standing in the middle of the street was his ward, Jamie Simmons. Sid reached out to the girl, as the freak had beckoned to him, but his voice was lost in the noise of the street below and the girl did not understand his gesture. She did not know who he was. She stood at the window, not moving, watching him. Then she cried out. Sid could not hear her, but he saw her face change, her mouth open. She raised her hands and held them beside her face. Then Sid saw her eyes close, then he heard some movement behind him, a whisper of something moving through the air.

Marcel sat in the front of the limousine with the driver. The back was empty. Anza had given over the hunt to Marcel. He trusted him, he knew Marcel would bring back the boy and the girl and the others who had betrayed him. Marcel was good at finding people who did not want to be found, as good as he was at persuading people to tell things they did not want to tell.

It was Marcel who had decided to come to the girl's apartment. Anza might have thought another move would bring the boy and the girl in more quickly, but he said nothing. He trusted Marcel's judgment. The Cuban had an instinct in such matters. If the girl did not return to the apartment, then someone would come who would lead Marcel to the girl and the boy and the cocaine.

Marcel had the driver go toward the center of town, to the address they had for the girl. Here the buildings were higher, the streets narrow, the traffic grew heavy. Marcel saw the red cab parked on the street before the girl's apartment. He had the driver pull the limousine in behind the cab. Marcel saw a man leaving the cab. The man was leaning forward, paying the driver, telling him to wait, Marcel thought. The man, a small muscular *güero*, got out of the cab and went into the girl's apartment building. After the man had gone into the building, the cab pulled away from the curb and went into the traffic. Perhaps the driver had not been told to wait after all. Marcel looked up at the building and saw nothing. He sat back and watched the entrance to the apartment. A minute or so passed and another red cab pulled into the space left by the first cab. The driver parked nearer the limousine than the first cab. The driver leaned forward, looking up at the surrounded buildings. Marcel looked up and saw the *güero*, the fair-haired man, standing at the windows in an apartment on the fifth or sixth floor. The girl's apartment. The man was looking down at the street, at the cab and the limousine. Marcel did not know who the fair-haired man was. He was not a cop, he was not one of those who had betrayed Anza.

The driver spoke to Marcel. A girl stood in the street, not five yards from the limousine. Marcel smiled. The girl they wanted was so close he could have opened the door and taken her away. But Marcel would wait. The girl was looking up at the fair-haired man in the window. The girl gave a cry, she called out a name, and ran onto the sidewalk and into the apartment building. A minute or so passed and the fair-haired man came running out of the building. He

121

crossed the street and went into the building opposite. Marcel looked at that building but could see nothing there. A minute, two minutes passed. Then Marcel saw the girl come to the window in the building above, where the fair-haired man had stood. The girl looked across the street, toward the building opposite. Still Marcel could see nothing there. Then the girl cried out and raised her hands as if in warning to someone in the building across the street. Then the girl Marcel wanted disappeared.

Marcel waited. His heart was pounding. It was happening too fast. There was too much he did not understand— the *güero*, the building across the way. He was about to speak to the driver, to get the girl now, when a man came out of the second building, the building opposite the girl's apartment. The man ran out of the building. He stopped abruptly on the sidewalk and looked up and down the street. The man saw the red cab and ran toward it. As he approached the cab Marcel saw it was not the *güero*. Marcel strained forward. In the instant when the cab door opened and the man leaped in the back, the cab's interior light came on. And Marcel saw the man's face. Marcel smiled. He said:

"Lex."

The driver turned the limousine into the traffic and went quickly after the red cab. The limousine followed the red cab for several blocks, then the car phone rang. Marcel picked up the receiver. Marcel listened, then he said in Spanish:

"I see. We do have him, Mr. Anza. . . .

—Lex.

—I see.

—Of course, Mr. Anza." And he put the phone away. Marcel spoke to the driver. "He has nothing," he said of the cab ahead. "We must find the girl again."

FOURTEEN

NOW every light was on in the apartment where Ash had been killed. The rooms were filled with men. Most of them were in the bathroom or in the hall looking into the bathroom, that was where the action was. In other places the boys from the lab were going over every hard surface for prints and the medical boys were standing around smoking and talking up the Dolphins, waiting for the photographers and the boys from the morgue to finish in the bathroom so they could take the stiff away, and there were the boys from the papers, Mal Berger had them standing out on the balcony, they were yelling questions and insults at Berger over the heads of the uniformed cops blocking the door. Berger had done his time in the bathroom. He had looked it over, seen everything he could see, and now he stood with

Dan Daniels, his partner, watching the lab boys go over the desk and the typewriter and the phone on the desk and the empty file folder that had been found under the desk. After the bathroom, the place of the murder, the desk and the small area around it were what most interested Mal Berger.

The lab boys finished with the desk. There was nothing there to find, maybe one good print on the file folder and some old prints on the typewriter case, but Mal Berger didn't think much would come of them. After the lab boys had moved on, Mal Berger went and sat at the chair before the desk. He turned to the typewriter and rolled a sheet of paper into the machine. He typed out a few words. He took the paper out of the machine, folded it and put it in his pocket. He lifted the phone and dialed a number. In time a man's voice came on the line.

"Harry, Mal Berger. Remember me—Homicide." Berger laughed at the man's reply.

"Yeah. Sorry about that, Harry. Something's come up. You know our bad egg? Somebody finally cracked him.

—Yeah. Ashburn. Over at his boyfriend's place.

—I don't know. Could be part of the Six Key thing. Lexington's up to his ass in that.

—Yeah, I guess Ash was too.

—I don't know, it doesn't feel right. Not yet.

—Nah, it wasn't the boyfriend. He's a cutter. Likes girls and kids. The guy who snuffed Ash ain't that kind of a freak.

—Yeah, the Colombians are out tonight, but it ain't them either.

—We found one of their pilots earlier. Jorgenson. Swede.

—That's him. Coulda been Six Key.

—Ash was garroted here in Lexington's apartment.

Head damned near taken off. The garrote was a blind cord taken from the apartment here.

—Well, you tell me, Harry—who likes rope?

—Yeah, I thought about that too. Some vet gone berserk. Only this don't seem that berserk.

—It has its moments, Harry. Ash was wearing rubber gloves—

—Right.

—Well, there's a typewriter open here on the desk. Portable. Still in the case. Maybe Ash brought it in. Maybe he was typing something he didn't want his prints on.

—There's more. There's a file folder here. An old one, from the Department. Empty.

—I don't know. There was talk Ash was putting the squeeze on somebody. Maybe Ash squeezed too hard. The guy met Ash, killed him and took whatever was in the folder.

—Well, there is one guy—a rich guy from New York. He showed up here today. But it ain't him.

—Mehring.

—Whatever you say, Harry, but he's got a lot of dough. Big money in New York.

—Harry, it'll be a pleasure to bust the motherfucker— if for no other reason than to get him out of my hair. But let me get the others too, Harry.

—You know who I'm talking about. The Racicot kid and this fucking Lex.

—All right, Harry, sir. But I got those two punks on the Six Key murder.

—Make it easy on yourself.

—Sure. On conviction. But the longer we let these two faggots run loose—

—Look, Harry, I understand who you got to deal with, but by morning every fucking Caddy trunk in Dade County could have a stiff in it.

—Okay, I'll wait. But warrants at ten. You're promising. Hang on a sec, Harry." Berger put his hand over the mouthpiece. Daniels had come up. Daniels said to Berger:

"Wald is here. You want to let him in?"

"Yeah, sure," said Berger, and Daniels went back toward the police guard at the door. Berger turned to the phone, swiveling the chair so that his back was to the apartment door and he wouldn't have to see Waldy when he came. "Wald just showed up. . . .

—You know, Ashburn's partner.

—Nah. He's a looker.

—I'll keep an eye on him. Nobody's clean tonight.

—Now for the cutie, Harry. Ash was found strangled, kneeling at the side of the tub in the bathroom. In the tub was a pile of white substance that the lab boys are going to check out, but I can tell you from my day off it's washing detergent. You know, you wash clothes in it. Twenty pounds of soap, the lab boys think.

—Beats the holy hell out of me. Ash had a gun on him, which he didn't use. The gun was found *in* the pile of detergent. And there was detergent on Ash's hands—on the rubber gloves.

—Well, for the love of Mike it looks like he was doing something in the soap, maybe trying to hide the gun, when the killer came up behind him and garroted him.

—Okay. I'll be in touch.

—Nah, I can handle it till morning. Just get me those goddamn warrants.

—Right, Chief. Hang on a sec, Harry." Daniels had come up to Berger. Berger put his hand over the receiver. Daniels said, "A couple calls you better take, Mal."

Berger took his hand off the receiver. "Business is looking up, Harry. Gotta go.

—Right. Bye."

Berger put down the phone. The morgue boys were rolling a carriage down the hallway, uniformed cops kicking back a couple of photographers who had bribed their way past the uniformed cops at the door. Ash's body was wrapped in a plastic sheet and strapped to the carriage. Waldy walked alongside the carriage looking like a relative mentioned in the will.

"Taking it hard, ain't he?" said Mal Berger and turned to Daniels. "What's up?"

"They found the other pilot. Swede's partner. Mike Davis. Same MO as Jorgenson."

"Davis. Yeah, he was a good one. Didn't he take out a bridge on the Yalu or something?"

"Vietnam. The war after ours, Mal."

Berger rubbed his chin. "Something else, Dan?"

"Yeah. This one might be fun. A call came in for Ash and it got transferred to us. From Felix Racicot. Says he's got the man who planned the Six Key murder at his place. Under force of arms, no less."

"Now who in the world would this be?"

"The guy from New York. Mehring."

Mal Berger stood. "All right. You got that warrant, Dan? Let's go and take a look at this New York asshole."

The two cops left the apartment and went onto the balcony. Some guy from PR was holding the boys from the newspapers at bay and the photographers had already left. Berger and Daniels went to their car without having to talk to anyone.

The floor was soft. Sid Mehring turned his face against it and felt nothing, nothing but the back of his head exploding every time his heart pumped. Sid came up to his knees and stayed there awhile. Even with his eyes closed he knew where he was. He could see the room with the mattresses on the floor and the table by the window. He could see the window and the apartment across the way and the girl crying out a warning he couldn't hear and didn't understand. He could even see the man coming up behind him, he could hear the slip of air the club or whatever it was made coming down on the back of his neck.

Sid came to his feet and went unsteadily across the mattresses. He sat at the chair at the table. He took up the telephone and dialed the number of his hotel. While the number was ringing Sid saw a small address book lying on the table. It had been left open at the R section.

The hotel operator came on the line.

"Sid Mehring. I've forgotten my room number. Messages?

—Lexington? What time?

—Say it again. I don't have a pen on me.

—817 New London. Apartment 201.

—Anything else?

—He knows who wrote the letters. I'll say the fuck he does.

—Sorry, operator. Just thinking out loud.

—Anything from New York?

—If anyone calls from New York, give them this message. I'll be at . . ." Sid lifted the address book that had been laid open on the table. "I'll be at Felix Racicot's house here in Miami. No street address. The Wells, it's called.

—Yes, that will be fine, operator. Thanks."

Sid put down the phone and rose. He went into the hall and pressed the elevator call button. As he waited a ragged purple face appeared from around the stairwell.

"Get him?" said the old man.

"He got me," Sid replied.

"Works that way sometimes," said the old man.

Sid took the elevator to the ground floor and went out onto the street. It was dark now, the long glowing evening had passed. All that moved and bore reflection glittered in the jungle of neon—the sleek passing cars, the walls and towers of glass and steel—everything shined and sparkled, either light or mirror.

Sid crossed the street. The cab was gone. Sid cursed but when he turned he saw the red cab approaching. He signaled and the cab pulled to the curb. Sid got in and told the driver the address of the Racicot mansion and the cab moved off through the traffic. As the cab went along Sid remembered something about the driver. His face, distorted under the curve of the windshield, looking up at Sid as he stood in the girl's window. The cab pulled to a stop before a traffic light and Sid moved forward in his seat.

"Driver, would you mind turning around to face me for a moment?"

"Sure, bud," said the driver and displayed the sorrowful mask of a clown, a pendulous nose, cheeks folded and hanging, a tidy mustache, twinkling close-set eyes. "I'm carrying a .45 if you're going to try something smart."

Sid moved back in the seat. "No. I had a different driver before. You all look alike—the cabs."

The cabbie shifted into gear and the cab moved forward. "Veterans' Cab Company. That's us. We ain't all vets, but it helps. You get priority. Me, I was a jarhead. World War Two. How 'bout you? You do any time?"

"Some."

"I thought so. You can spot 'em. Vets. Which branch?"

"Army."

"That's okay. Vietnam, I bet. Officer. Captain. Am I right?"

"You're right. Do you know where you're going?"

"Me? I thought you did," said the cabbie and showed

his wrinkled face and some mock worry. Then the cabbie grinned and went back to looking at the street occasionally. "Just kidding. Sure, I know the place. The Wells House. The Racicot place. Right? Am I right? Pretty high cotton. But that's okay. Some of these rich guys—they deserve it. They didn't earn it—that's not what I mean. I am more of your liberal-type person. But some of these rich guys, like Racicot, the way they wear all their dough. It fits. It works. All that dough, it's natural to them. You know what I mean? Like being a socialist-type person is natural to me."

"You're sure you know where we're going?"

"Sure I'm sure. I'm talking too much. I know. I'll shut up." There was a moment's silence. "You know, I ain't really got a .45. Not on me, anyway. I got it at home. If I get a call out to my neighborhood I think I'll stop by and pick it up. It's a nasty night out there tonight. Fucking battleground. Three stiffs already and it ain't ten o'clock. That's what the dispatcher says. He's plugged into the police band. Two trunk jobs. Drug stuff. White guys. Pilots. Then a cop got it. Some narc. Over in the Grove. It's a nasty one, tonight is. And then one of our own is missing. Cab and driver both. Now I ain't saying Rudy has been snuffed. He gets a little strange sometimes. Pulled a trick and took off on his own, maybe. Nothing that a jab at the doc's won't cure. But you never can be too careful. If the cops don't get their ass in gear, me and a couple other drivers are gonna come together. You know, get our pieces and start taking care of our own."

"You know, I do have a headache."

"Yeah, sure. Sure. I get you. Fine. Okay." There was a short silence. "You want some soap?"

"Soap?"

"Yeah. You know. Laundry detergent. Soap. For the little lady." The cabbie reached under his seat and brought out a small box of detergent, while honking, braking and swerving to miss a Caddy that had changed lanes without signaling. "Some guy with his nose packed," said the cabbie, dangling the box of soap over the seat. "Free sample, see. They're hanging them on all the doorknobs all over town. The winos. You've seen them walking around with these satchels."

"I'm not sure that I have," Sid said, taking the offered box, if only to free the cabbie's hand for steering or shifting gears and things like that.

"Ah, you have, you just ain't noticed. They're all over town. Now, some of the guys, they go along and take the stuff off the doorknobs while people ain't home. I'm not into that, as a liberal sort of person. But Jesus Christ, these winos are dumping this shit in every culvert and dumpster in town. By the case. They get tired of hauling this crap around. The dispatcher he ain't checking too close, the winos dump as much as they hang. Now I'm driving along, minding my own business and see this case—the whole fucking case, forty boxes—and I stop my cab and open the door and it hops right in. What am I to say, as an anarchist sort of person?"

Sid sat forward in the seat and looked about. The cab had come to a stop. The cabbie was turned back toward Sid, his hand open, palm up. There was nothing for miles around but night and willow draped with Spanish moss.

"This is it," said the cabbie. "The Wells. Felix Racicot's place. Take my word for it. Right through there. Kinda spooky, ain't it?"

Sid looked. He could see nothing but dark and haunted trees. "You're sure?"

The cabbie peered into the dark. Moss fell in streams from the trees like rocks bleeding from cavern walls. "I'm pretty sure."

Sid got out of the cab. He drew a bill from his pocket. "I want you to wait for me. All right?"

"Wait here?" said the cabbie.

"Right. This is not going to take long." Sid gave the cabbie the bill. The cabbie looked at it.

"This is a C-note," the cabbie said.

"That's right. And it's got a twin if you're here when I come out. And there's going to be another hundred for the next place I want to go. And so on. I need a friend tonight. You're going to be my friend. Right?"

"Right. I'm not scared."

Sid took several strides into the dark and the cabbie called out:

"And keep the soap. Compliments of the cab."

Sid saw he still had the sample box in his hand. He turned and tossed the box into the dark and went on toward a faint light he could see through the trees.

Felix Racicot gazed at the painting of the man and woman as he waited for Lex's call to come through. He had bought the picture long before the artist died, long before his fame, long before musuems from Berlin to New York had come begging to include this oil in their collections. Felix Racicot had bought this painting long before it became the most valuable single object in his possession. A man's voice came on the line and Felix Racicot turned away from the thing he loved most in the world, save perhaps for his son. As Felix Racicot turned away from the painting he took up a decanter filled with a green liqueur and held it to the light.

"Yes. Felix Racicot speaking.

—No, of course. I don't mind your calling at all. I

understand these things often don't work out as we have planned them.

—I've been following it on television.

—Oh, I'm sure it wasn't such a botch as they make it seem. They do have their viewers to entertain.

—Ah, dear me! Were you injured?

—I knew, of course, that Mr. Mehring could be a dangerous man, but I didn't dream he would be so violent. At least not out of his uniform.

—No, Jimmy can handle things here. I'm quite sure of that.

—Ah well, thank you so very much for telling me he's coming.

—Of course, I understand. I know how you feel about my son. And he is, shall we say, devoted to you.

—That soon?" said Felix Racicot, looking at his wristwatch. "Well then, we do have much to do before Mr. Mehring arrives, don't we?

—Yes. Thank you, Lex. Goodbye.

—And good luck to you."

Felix Racicot broke the connection, then dialed a single number that rang a phone in another part of the house. A man answered.

"Jimmy, will you please get Mother's room ready now?

—Yes. Just as we spoke of. With the tent and the tanks—just as it was when she died. Let's have flowers, Jimmy. That would be nice.

—Yes. And some whites for you and Marie. There must be something around.

—All this must be done quickly, Jimmy. I've been informed Mr. Mehring's on his way.

—Yes. Exactly. Now, please listen carefully, Jimmy. When Mr. Mehring arrives he and I will be shown into the

133

sickroom. Briefly. Then we will come to the library. As soon as we are in the library I want you to call the number I gave you and ask for Detective Sergeant Ashburn. Tell him the man who planned the Six Key murder is here.

—Exactly. Are you armed, Jimmy?

—Good. Mr. Mehring is a dangerous and violent man. We should be ready for anything.

—Now, can you think of anything else, Jimmy?

—Oh no no, I'll be quite all right. There's nothing that Mr. Mehring—or anyone—can do to me now.

—Ah well, Jimmy, that is very kind. Thank you very much."

Felix Racicot broke the connection and dialed an outside number. A man answered.

"Warren? Felix Racicot here.

—I'm very sorry to have disturbed you at this hour, Warren, but I'm afraid the contingency I spoke to you about has occurred.

—I'm afraid so. I must have the money tonight.

—Yes, an hour will be fine. But no later."

The man on the line then spoke at some length. As the man went on Felix Racicot poured a small glass of the green liqueur from the bottle. He raised the liqueur to his nose and smiled, a bit uncertainly, as if the scent of the liqueur brought forth a sad memory. He cradled the thimble of liqueur in his hand as the man on the line concluded.

"Thank you, Warren. I know that everything you say is correct, but there are—

—Yes, Warren. But there are times in a man's life when logic and legal reasoning, when the very concepts of right and wrong, are meaningless. There are times when even the distinction between life and death blur."

Felix Racicot laughed, genuinely amused. "Do I really sound as bad as all that?" Felix Racicot smiled at the well-meaning coming from the other man. At length he broke into the man's monologue:

"Yes, I understand. All that is perfectly clear, Warren, but still could you please bring the money tonight—in an hour, no later. Perhaps we can discuss the point then.

—No, I'm afraid not, Warren. I must go now. An hour. Till then."

Felix Racicot put down the phone, placed the glass of liqueur on a table nearby and left the library. His face was set now, his look at once determined and vague, as if his mind were preoccupied with a puzzle he could not solve. He went along the corridor to another door, knocked and went in without waiting for a reply. His son sat slouched in a chair, flipping through a magazine, looking both bored and afraid, like a patient in a doctor's anteroom. When the boy's father entered the room the magazine slid from his hands and the boy grasped the arms of the chair as if his father had come to take him away. The man approached the boy and knelt by his chair. A look of disgust formed on the boy's face. When the father reached out to touch his son, the boy pulled his hand away.

"Mehring is on his way now," said Felix Racicot. "It will all be over soon. I will take care of them all." A smile slid across the boy's face and he turned away from his father. Felix Racicot stood, that he would not be tempted to embrace his son. "I want you to go to Mother's room now. Jimmy and Marie are there. You must undress and get into bed. When Mehring and I come in you must—"

"Look sick?" The boy sniggered.

"You must pretend to be asleep. Jimmy will give you something to make it easier if you like."

"No, no," said the boy, disturbed, waving his hand. "I don't want anything. I don't need it. I'll be going out later."

"By, you've got to stay here. Even with Sergeant Ashburn as a friend, you must have this alibi."

The boy whirled in the chair, his face streaked with fear. "Don't tell me how to handle this! I'm in charge! I'm in charge here!" He turned away, twisting one hand in the other, a frightened child.

Felix Racicot knelt by his son. He touched him. The boy did not pull away. "You can do what you want, By. You can have anything you want. I've spoken to Warren. He's coming with the money. You can do whatever you want with it. It's yours."

There came a small sound from the boy: "Thank you, Daddy. Thank you."

The phone across the room rang, a soft bell, like the purr of a cat. Felix Racicot went to it and took up the receiver.

"Yes.

—Already? Keep him downstairs for a moment. I'll be there shortly. Are you in whites, Jimmy?

—Good. When I come down, please come up and help Byron to Mother's room. Bring the wheelchair. And when you move him, Jimmy, try not to wake him," said Felix Racicot, for in those few moments his son had fallen asleep, his head resting on the arm of the chair. "He looks so at peace now."

Sid Mehring did not like the picture. It was not his cup of tea. His mother would have said that or something like it and she would have been right. The man and the woman were naked. There was nothing erotic in their nakedness, nor was there meant to be. Or so it seemed at first, that the artist had meant nothing more than to present flesh as meat, sex as hunger. The woman lay on her back on the floor, only the trunk of her body visible, her feet and her head and face and her arms, which looked to be resting behind her head, extending beyond the frame of the painting. The man was seated on the floor beside the woman, cross-legged, bent over slightly, studying the woman's body laid out before him. The man was ordinary-looking, thin, with short dark hair and thick dark-rimmed glasses and a shadowy day's growth of beard. The man looked bemused, gazing uncertainly at the woman's body, as if he did not know what purpose it was intended to serve. His genitals hung limp, with equal disinterest. The woman had been painted even less kindly. She had large loose breasts that fell over her chest and draped cruelly, stretching the skin covering them. The woman's pubic hair was reddish blond and grew scantily. The flesh of both man and woman was a stark white, flesh that had never seen sun. Sid had never seen anything quite so clearly as he saw these bodies, not his own body nor the body of any lover. And if the artist's intentions had not been made perfectly clear, he had painted a leg of beef or mutton placed on a platter in the picture's foreground. The meat was raw and red. So far as Sid was concerned this leg of lamb or whatever it was did for cuisine what the woman's body did for sex. Looking at the picture, Sid Mehring was decidedly without appetite, of any sort.

Sid was even less taken with Felix Racicot, who stood by the mantel, looking up with adulation at the picture. Racicot was a slender man, in his fifties, elegant in speech, dress and manner; charming, worldly, casually knowledge-able in a number of fields—cybernetics, the gold market, Italy—that were of some interest to Sid Mehring. In fact, so brilliant and well informed was Felix Racicot that Sid Mehring thought he might have passed for a wise man. But Felix Racicot was not wise—so Sid Mehring thought as he watched the man inhale the bouquet of a small glass of liqueur—he was foolish. And he was weak and vain and arrogant. And he was afraid. He was afraid of all the things he knew so well—genius, power and cunning. And he was, above all, at this very moment, as he handed Sid Mehring a glass of liqueur and moved away from the nasty painting, afraid of Sid Mehring.

The two men had come to the library from the sickroom, where Sid Mehring had been first taken. There, in the the sickroom, Sid Mehring had been shown the boy lying unconscious in bed, the oxygen tent and tanks, the flowers, the nurses, a man and a woman, hovering about. Then Racicot and Sid had left quietly, the boy's father on tiptoe. Sid Mehring had believed that show just about as much as he believed the painting the man adored was a masterpiece. They had come to this room, the library, and here had spoken of the painting and of other things, but now they had finished with that and they turned to those matters that were really on their minds.

Felix Racicot stood at the broad French windows that looked out over the front grounds of his estate. The grounds were dark.

"How did you come, Mr. Mehring? By car?"

"I took a cab."

"I see. I saw a light on the road. Could it be your driver?"

"I asked him to wait."

"I see," said Felix Racicot and came away from the window and spoke directly to Sid Mehring: "My son had nothing to do with the Six Key affair, you know."

Sid placed the vile-smelling liqueur on a table at hand, untouched. "Didn't he?"

Felix Racicot frowned. "Byron—what is the term?—

my son overdosed last Friday, Mr. Mehring. He's been under the care of Dr. Jonah Steinhart since. I have Dr. Steinhart's number here somewhere, if you care to call him." Sid made a gesture of dismissal. "He has the most ironclad of alibis—I assure you. It would have been impossible for Byron to have been involved in the Six Key—murders, I suppose they are calling them now. Nor could he have been party to the drug smuggling and the burn—is that the word?—that seems to have precipitated these terrible killings."

"Racicot, how the fuck do you know why I have come to see you?"

Felix Racicot seemed pained. "I have a friend—a contact—in the Miami Police Department. He has called and told me of your presence in Miami. Why you are here and why you suspect—erroneously—that my son had something to do with these killings."

"Jim Ashburn?"

Felix Racicot inclined his head to one side, as if the pain were worse there. He moved across the room and took a chair opposite Sid Mehring. He moved the dram of liqueur under his nose, the small glass never leaving his hand. He acknowledged Sid Mehring's question with a nod and spoke sorrowfully in evading it.

"Alas, my son does take drugs. He is even addicted or habitually uses a great deal of cocaine and amphetamines. And of course they all smoke cannabis. But Byron would never produce or smuggle or sell these drugs. Byron is incapable of doing anything that would take that much will or courage. I love my son more than my own life, Mr. Mehring, but he is a child in this world. He is much like me in this. Men who will remain children so long as we live."

"What crap, Racicot," Sid Mehring said. "Your son flies, right?"

"Flies?"

"Yeah. Flies." Sid Mehring moved his hand through the air as boys and pilots do. "Airplanes. In the sky."

"Yes. He's a very good pilot. Good at propelling all sorts of machines—boats, cars and airplanes."

"If he can fly, Racicot, he's capable of smuggling. That's all you need. Not courage or will." Sid Mehring took a ballpoint pen from his pocket and worked the button five or six times, as if he might go on doing so all night. "All right. You tell me, Racicot—what happened? What's your theory? Why have I been told by the Miami police, by your pal Jim Ashburn, that your son—in a coma since last Friday, right?—why is it that Sergeant Ashburn tells me that not only did your son pull off some smuggling heist and burn the Colombians he was working for, not only that but that he has also murdered two people, with extreme cruelty and some forethought, so that it would appear that he and my ward Jamie Simmons died in a car crash at Six Key Cut? If your worthless son has been in a coma since Friday, why has your buddy Ashburn given me this song and dance, Racicot?"

Felix Racicot put down the glass of liqueur. He held his hands together. They quivered like rabbits before a snake. "Ashburn was not the contact I meant. I know someone else with the police."

"Fuck. Who told you what isn't the point, is it? The point is that the Miami police have given me one hypothesis —that your son was up to his ass in Six Key Cut—and now I'd like to hear yours."

The telephone in the room rang, and Felix Racicot went to it. "Oh yes, Jimmy," the man said into the receiver. "Now would be the perfect time to call. Thank you, Jimmy." Felix Racicot put down the phone. He left his hand on the receiver, as if he were about to take it up again and make another call. He turned and came back to Sid Mehring. He took the chair opposite Sid and gazed at the canvas over the mantel. "If you must know, the center of Six Key is found deep within the nature of your ward—Miss Simmons. It is not a pretty picture, Mr. Mehring."

Sid scowled at the meat painting. "I'll bet."

Felix Racicot smiled. "What do you think of faces, Mr. Mehring?"

"It depends on the face."

"Exactly. Most faces are like that, aren't they? We use them as guides to the minds and the hearts of the men and the women who live behind them. Who was it who said faces were windows to the soul?"

"I forget."

"It's not a very accurate image in any case. I prefer to think of the face as the skin on a soul. It lies over what is deepest and most secret within us—our loves, fears, dreams, our ambitions and our hatreds—and though it protects these things, as skin protects flesh, it also follows the forms of all these secret things, just as skin follows the form of the flesh and bone. This is true of us all, I think, or almost all. You have looked at me, Mr. Mehring, and have decided that I am a weak, desperate man who will do anything to save my son. And while looking at you, I have come to the conclusion you are a rich, arrogant bastard from New York who can be led ring-a-rosy long enough for my contact with the Miami police, Jim Ashburn, to arrive so that we may decide together what to do with you. Correct?"

Sid shifted in the chair. "Close enough."

"But then you and I, with our reflective appearances, are not the point. There is another sort of person with another sort of face. A young woman, a girl when I first met her, scarcely in her teens. Her youth and beauty and innocence, Mr. Mehring, above all goodness, glowed in the face of Jamie Simmons when I first saw her. It was only gradually, over the years, that I came to see the evil and the cruelty shielded by her youth and beauty. But by then it was too late to save my son. He was lost to this girl's deception no matter what I could say or do." Felix Racicot halted a moment, then came out of his reverie. "You've never met your ward, have you, Mr. Mehring?"

"Not face to face," said Sid Mehring with a sneer.

"Just as well. She loathes you, Mr. Mehring. She always has. From the very first. I believe Jamie Simmons came to be your ward because of some accident in the war—her only surviving relative, her brother, died saving your life. Is that correct?"

"Yes."

"Ah there. You see? From the very first she twisted this truth so that some sort of negligence on your part was the cause of Sergeant Simmons's death. She turned heroism and self-sacrifice into sloth and cowardice. And she continued to loathe you, Mr. Mehring. She loathed you even more as you took her under your financial wing and provided for her so generously. She came to despise the life you lead, the work you do, and the society which produces men like you, and me."

Sid Mehring grinned and didn't speak.

Felix Racicot lowered his head. "I know what I am saying sounds harsh to you, Mr. Mehring, but this girl has ruined my son, with her drugs and lawlessness and her sex." The man looked up to the meat picture, then took his eyes away. "These murders, these unspeakable crimes that she and her mentor have committed—I only wish she did have parents, a family, someone to suffer as I have done."

Sid Mehring kept grinning. "My ward has an evil mentor, Racicot?"

"Yes. A man named Lexington." Racicot stood and

looked about the room as if he were lost there, in his own house. "He was their . . . drug pusher? Dealer? You must forgive me. I feel so foolish using these words. This man, Lex, they called him, he sold them drugs when my son and your ward were in high school. When they were indeed Romeo and Juliet. Perhaps I was at fault. I'm sure I was— letting them taste life so fully so young. I knew that their lovemaking and their experiments with drugs were wrong, conventionally, legally, morally, but I sanctioned them. It was in part a reaction against my own youth, a youth spent without any of these pleasures. I lived my youth in theirs, a terrible error for a father to make. I blinded myself to what mindless sensual gratification does to one's spirit and to one's character. I loathed my father, Mr. Mehring, but I was so wrong to loathe his teaching. If I grew up hearing of nothing but right and wrong, they came of age knowing the meaning of neither. Children of Dionysus, Mr. Mehring. Fertile soil for the seeds of Mr. Lexington, a dope pusher, a thief, a homosexual brutalizer, a murderer and a torturer. Lex initiated Byron and the girl into his world. By had no defenses against him. Drugs, abnormal sex, crime—life had been reduced to sensation. An act was judged merely by stimulation. Whatever turned them on, Mr. Mehring.

"But then there was something in Byron—bloodline, I would like to think, but more likely it was simply fear that made him draw back." Felix Racicot had come to a stop in his wandering about the rom. He stood before the tall windows looking out over the front grounds. "You say you came in a taxi, Mr. Mehring? What color is it?"

"Red."

"Ah, that explains it," said Felix Racicot, turning from the window. "I saw a light and it was so red." The man came to the chair opposite Sid Mehring. Now his feminine, patrician grace was gone. He sat forward, his elbows resting

143

on his legs, looking at the floor. "What I'm going to tell you now I've never told another living being. What I've said before was nothing—what I'm going to tell you now is the truth." He raised his head and looked across the room. "About a year ago, this time a year ago, they murdered a man. They tortured him to death. He was a small-time drug dealer—a boy, I suppose, not twenty years old. He cheated them, in some way. They—Lexington tortured the boy to death. I don't know what Jamie or Byron did or didn't do, Mr. Mehring. But they were there. They watched it done, at the very least. Byron came to me and told me about the murder. He was still drugged. He had to be to do what he had done. He confessed, he told me exactly how it had happened. What they had done. He pleaded with me to save him. And I did. I saved my son and his murderous friends from justice. You must understand that I did not think of myself as an accessory to this hideous crime. Not then. Not the first time. I truly thought I was doing right. And good. And that the horror of what they had done would change them, that it would make them see that it was their lives that were wrong. But then, Mr. Mehring, one morning several months later I lifted my paper and there, on the front page, was the story of another brutal torture slaying. Committed, the writer speculated, by the same madmen who had done the previous murder. But that writer was wrong, you see," said Racicot with a wisp of a smile. "It was I who killed the second boy. I am the murderer you want, Mr. Mehring."

Sid Mehring waited while the man wept. Then he said: "You finished, Racicot? I have to give you credit. It's one of the worst acting jobs I've ever seen. The whole setup, everything about this place, you and your stories, it's all—what would be a genteel, old-fashioned word that might get through to you? It's all *hooey*, Racicot. There's no fucking evil genius named Lex at the bottom of this. He was invented for me by your pal Ashburn. And your son's not sick—oh, he's sick, all right, but another sick, one that nurses with grease under their nails and empty oxygen tanks can't touch. It's all bullshit. Like this picture. You figure you paint people as ugly as you can make them look and that's the truth? Well, it's not. All that sagging skin is just as fake as a *Playboy* foldout. What's in this is you and your worthless son and this slimy cop Ashburn. Now let's talk about that, Racicot."

The phone rang, purring. "I suppose we could, Mr. Mehring," said Felix Racicot. He leaned his head toward the phone. "Do you mind?"

Sid Mehring looked away. "Answer the fucking thing."

Felix Racicot went to the phone. As he crossed the room he pulled a revolver from his jacket pocket. He continued to speak in his calm, philosophical manner. "Perhaps I have been less than candid with you, Mr. Mehring, but I have told you one thing that is true. To love someone evil is to become evil." The man raised the receiver to his ear. "Ah, at long last. Thank you, Jimmy. Yes, would you please show them up," said Felix Racicot and turned the gun on Sid Mehring.

Berger and Daniels left the city and the sea and went inland. As they went the sky closed over them, overcast; a ground fog came up and swirled around the unmarked car. The palms of the beach gave way to cypress and willow and mangrove, all draped with gray webs of moss. The houses became old and dark and quiet here, in this part of town, away from the crazed cluster of neon and cars and tourists and freaks of the city. Here the streets were narrow, winding, like country lanes, though the cops knew there were houses and people here, set back off the streets. The houses of the rich. And then beyond this were the houses of the poor clinging to the edge of the swamp and beyond that just swamp and fog and dark.

The cops saw the red cab parked off the road and pulled in behind it. They would have been lost without the cab, the street they had come on had grown so narrow and uneven and overhung with willow and moss, the houses set so far back from the street they might have been following a track through the swamp. The cabbie had been reading inside the cab, and he got down low in the seat when the car pulled in behind his. When he saw it was an unmarked cop car, the cabbie got out. The cops got out of their car and laughed at the cabbie with the clown's face.

The cabbie waved his *Racing Form* at the cops. "You assholes! We lost one of our boys tonight, cab and all. Rudy Mahalevich! Whatta you doing about that?"

The cops started walking away, through the willow and hanging moss, toward a distant light. "What are you doing out here anyway, Sherman, in the middle of the fucking night?"

"I got a fare, Daniels, and don't you fuck with him!"

The cops laughed and went on walking. They found a wide gravel path and could see a huge house in the distance and a light over a door. The cops went up the path, their shoes crackling on the gravel. They went up the steps and across a deep, colonnaded porch and knocked on the door. A man dressed in whites swung back the door.

"Detectives Berger and Daniels," said Mal Berger to the man in white. "You called?"

"Sergeant Ashburn isn't with you?"

"He got tied up tonight," said Mal Berger, walking past the man in white. "We've come to make an arrest. You want to let us in?"

"Certainly, sir." The man in white turned and spoke into a phone beside the door. He then came around the two cops and led them into the house.

Mal Berger looked about as they went into the house. They had been let into a wide hall, fifty feet long, illuminated only by light from a room at its end. On either side as they went down the hall were double doors, closed now, but leading, Mal Berger imagined from the doors' size, into immense flanking rooms. Berger saw at the end of the hall a spiral stair that led to the upper reaches of the house. The stair was as dark as the hall, illuminated only by lights coming from the rooms above. As they reached the stairs Berger saw that the open door beneath the stairs led into a narrow, white-lacquered hall and, he imagined, to the kitchen and utility rooms at the back of the ground floor of the house. The floor of the hall and the stairs was some stone, waxed and polished, and the heels of the cops' shoes cracked against the hard surface as they crossed the hall and climbed the stairs.

The cops and the servant in white went up the stairs to a second-story landing. They crossed a foyer and went along a hall that led in the direction they had come, toward the front of the house. They came to double doors like those below. The man in white knocked lightly on one of the doors and let the two cops into a spacious room filled with books and comfortable furniture and objects of art and memorabilia, all suffused with warm light from the lamps placed about the room. Across the room was a fireplace and mantel and some piece of modern art hanging above them. At the far end of the room were French windows that looked down on the front grounds of the house. Two men sat in chairs flanking the fireplace. One man held a gun on the other, though it seemed the men might have been chatting amiably when the servant had tapped on the door. The floor of the

147

room and the hall the cops had just come down were covered with rugs, rugs over rugs, as if to compensate for the barren floor below. Here the two cops came into the library and went across it without making a sound.

Mal Berger went to the man who held the gun. By the look on Felix Racicot's face—shock and worry—Mal Berger would have thought it was the other man who had the gun trained on him. Mal Berger slid the gun from Felix Racicot's hand. Berger grinned.

"Mr. Racicot? I'm sorry that Sergeant Ashburn couldn't answer your call personally, but he's been murdered tonight." Berger turned to the other man. "Sid Mehring?"

The small, hard, sandy-haired man grinned. "That's right."

"I'm placing you under arrest."

Sid Mehring stood, still grinning. Berger turned to Daniels. "I don't believe there's any need to put cuffs on this gentleman, is there, Dan?"

Daniels took Mehring's arm and they went out of the room. Berger turned to Racicot. A rigid smile had come to Racicot's face. Berger said, "Thank you for your citizenship, sir, in helping apprehend this man."

Racicot looked at the cop, distracted. His gaze went past Berger to the painting above the mantel. Berger viewed the painting. Man, woman, mutton—he had known they were all meat all along. He turned to Racicot. "We were wondering, sir, if you have had any other threats on your life tonight."

Racicot had picked up a dram of green liqueur. "Threats? No. Nothing."

"Well, in any case, Mr. Racicot, a police officer has been murdered tonight and though we think we have his killer, we can never be sure." He offered the gun he had taken from Racicot. "Just in case."

Racicot looked at the gun in the cop's hand. "Yes, of course. Put it down. Anywhere."

Berger put the gun on a table near Racicot. "Goodnight, sir. And be sure to give us a ring if you have any more trouble. My number." Berger put his card by the pistol.

"Thank you, officer," said the man. "Would you care to join me in a drink?"

"No thank you, sir. Not on duty."

Racicot smiled. "Of course."

"Goodnight, sir," said Mal Berger and left Felix Racicot with the small glass balanced in his hand.

Berger went downstairs and out the front. The servant in white had disappeared. He saw no one else around. Daniels was loading Mehring into the back when he got to the car. Berger reached in for the radio mike. The cabbie was standing at the front of the cab, the cab between him and the cops.

"What the hell are you doing with my fare, Berger? It was going to be the best night I ever had!"

Berger called headquarters and then got in the car. Daniels was already in the driver's seat, Sid Mehring in the back. Daniels turned the car and they went back through the hanging moss and mist and dark.

Berger turned to the man in the back. "Mehring, you want to tell us what the fuck you're doing down here?"

Sid looked at the cop with disdain, his hands folded under his arms. "I'm going to have your ass and your badge for this bust."

"You are?" Berger grinned at Daniels and took a folded paper from his jacket. "We got a warrant for you, Mehring."

"Bullshit. I didn't have a fucking thing to do with Ashburn's murder and you know it."

Berger grinned at his partner. "Did I say anything

149

about murder, Dan?" He unfolded the warrant. "Traffic violations. Stationary. One hundred and thirty-seven counts. The City of New York is going to extradite you in the morning, Mehring."

Sid Mehring sneered. "Those aren't my parking tickets. They're my chauffeur's."

The cops laughed.

Daniels drove to the downtown station and went into the parking garage beneath the building. Two uniformed cops met them and took custody of Sid Mehring. The four cops and Mehring rode the elevator to the booking section on the second floor. As the clerk was interviewing Sid Mehring, Berger took one of the uniformed cops aside.

"Let the New York wiseass make his call before you process him, Jerry. Dan and I will be down in room eleven. Put it in there on the speaker. And Jerry, kid gloves with the guy. Put him someplace quiet."

The uniformed cop went to the desk, where Sid Mehring was emptying his pockets and the clerk itemizing the contents. Berger took a cup of coffee and went down a hall to a room that was bare but for a table and three chairs. There was a one-way mirror in the back wall; it looked into an empty holding cell. A clock and an amplified speaker hung on another wall. Berger switched on the speaker and took a chair and sipped his coffee. In a few moments Daniels came in and sat across from Berger. He did not look happy.

"They found the cabbie, Mal. Rudy Mahalevich. Garroted, like Ash."

"Fuck. In his cab?"

"Nah. The cab is gone. Some bum found the body down by Shu's. Where they were going to put the new freeway through."

"The paper-hanging place."

"Right. This is beginning to give me the heebies, Mal.

Two Colombian jobs and then this strangler on the fucking loose."

Mal Berger rubbed the flesh of his face and his scalp and the back of his neck, working the muscles with his big hands. He started to speak, but the amplified speaker crackled. Sid Mehring's voice came on the speaker.

"Operator, I want to call New York City collect." Sid Mehring gave a number and the call went through. A man accepted the call. Sid Mehring said, "Dick, this is Sid. Is Margot there?"

The man's voice was wary. "Here? I thought she was there."

"What do you mean here?"

"There. Where are you?"

"I'm in jail, Dick."

"What are you doing in jail?"

"Parking violations. Dick, where is Margot?"

"There. With you. Aren't you in Miami?"

"Why is Margot in Miami?"

"Actually, she's probably not there yet. She left about three hours ago."

"Why is Margot coming to Miami, Dick?"

"Your ward called."

"Jamie Simmons?"

"Yes. She called earlier in the evening. She was in trouble. Not dead. Like you figured. Margot thought she'd fly down and straighten things out."

"Right. What time does her flight get in?"

"She should be coming in anytime now."

"Jesus. Dick, what's the name of that law firm down here? Finley something. Get hold of Finley and get me the hell out of this place."

"Are you really in jail?"

"Dick."

151

"Anything else?"

"Just a second, Dick." Sid Mehring spoke off the line: "Would you say again, officer. Thank you. Just finishing up." He came back to the line: "My three minutes are up. I've got to have my picture taken. Do me a favor, Dick, tomorrow morning take Jerzy down to wherever these things are done and pay whatever parking fines he owes."

"Okay. Anything else?"

"Get me out of here."

"Two hours max. Goodnight, Sid."

The line went dead, and Mal Berger turned off the speaker. He turned to his partner. "What do you think we got here, Dan?"

"Well, the Colombian jobs look like the Six Key burn and I thought maybe Ash was too. But the cabbie don't fit."

Mal Berger rubbed the back of his neck. "Jesus, maybe I need to get some glasses or something. My head is killing me." Berger yawned. "My old lady says I'm just getting fat and I need new shirts. Collar's too tight." He put his head back against the chair. "Mahalevich was a freak. Maybe he had something to do with the death car out at the Cut. Maybe he procured the lady wino."

"You know, a call came in about the lady wino. A bartender downtown. She remembered the woman. She was in the joint last night. Then tonight there was some guy in there looking for her."

Mal Berger sat up. "Who was looking for her?"

"Don't know." Daniels went through his pockets. He brought a memo slip. "The Firefly. Downtown."

Mal Berger pulled his tie to his collar. "Let's have a beer, Dan."

* * *

The banker counted the packets of one-hundred-dollar bills, taking them out of the case and placing them on the table, arranging them in the same low rectangle they had made in the case. When he had done this, the banker counted the bills again, replacing them in the case. Neat, counting everything twice, it was why Felix Racicot trusted Warren, why he knew he could ask Warren to bring three hundred thousand dollars in one-hundred-dollar bills to his house in the middle of the night. The banker looked at the neatly packaged money and then closed the case. The banker snapped the latches and kept his hands on the case.

"Felix."

"Warren, don't you have something for me to sign?"

The banker released the case and took a sheath of papers and laid them out, copy after copy, on the table. He came along behind as Felix Racicot signed the documents, picking them up. When the documents had been signed and retrieved the two men stood facing one another, the case between them.

"I don't suppose there's any point in telling you what a terrible mistake this is."

"No."

"You're a fool, Felix, to think this will solve anything."

"I know."

The banker took one of the signed documents and placed it under the corner of the case. He then turned and left the room, not making a sound, as he had come to the Racicot mansion in some sort of jogging suit, with rubber-soled shoes.

Felix Racicot waited till he heard the sound of the front door close, then he took the case and went into the hall and climbed the spiral stairs to the second floor. There he went along a hall toward the rear of the house. He came to a door and opened it quietly. A light burned in one corner

153

of the room; in another was a hospital bed. An oxygen tank and a display of flowers stood by the bed. Byron Racicot lay in the bed, his back to his father. Felix Racicot went across the room without making a sound. He placed a hand on the boy's shoulder and said, "By."

The boy mumbled in his sleep and turned on his back. His face was blotched, puffed. His eyes turned to the ceiling, vacant, uncomprehending.

"By, they're gone now. All of them. I've got the money."

The boy's head turned toward his father. "You're alone?" The boy sat up and looked about the room. He swung his legs from under the sheet and sat up. He wore trousers beneath his pajama tops, and shoes. The boy leaned toward his father and Felix Racicot placed his arms around the boy and held him. Then he felt the boy go cold under his embrace and he saw the boy's eyes were turned toward the case. The boy reached out and touched the case as Felix Racicot had once touched the boy. "How much did you get?" he said.

"Not all of it. I couldn't get all of it tonight."

"How much did you get?"

"Three hundred thousand."

"That's all right, Daddy. Thank you." The boy took up the case and held it.

"I'll get the rest in the morning, when the banks open. It will take some work, paperwork, two or three days. But this should buy us the time we need."

The boy was not listening. He stood and looked about the room. "Where's my jacket?"

The man stood before the boy. He reached for the case. "Let me make the transfer. Let me deal with these men. I know them. I can talk to them."

The boy's eyes went about the room. "Where's my jacket?"

The man turned aside. "On the bed."

When the man turned back the boy had put on the jacket. He stood in the center of the room, his arms about the case. "What time is it, Daddy?"

"Almost midnight."

The boy looked at his father. "Thank you, Daddy, thank you for this. Lex is coming for me. We'll take it to them. He knows these men, Daddy. He's the one who knows how to do this. Not you, Daddy. I don't want you to get hurt, don't you see?"

The boy moved toward his father as if to embrace him, but he still held the case in his arms. Felix Racicot turned away from his son, as if to straighten the bed covers. "Ash was murdered tonight."

"Ash?"

"They found him in Lex's apartment. Strangled." Felix Racicot looked back, but his son's attention had gone away from him. He stood facing in another direction, listening.

Felix Racicot heard the distant sound, the horn of a car playing a note.

"I've got to go, Daddy," the boy said and went through the door.

Felix Racicot pulled the bed cover so that it was straight. He went out the door and down the hall to the library. There he crossed to the French windows looking over the front grounds of the house. Felix Racicot saw that the red cab—the one that had brought Sid Mehring, he supposed—had pulled onto the gravel walk that led from the street to the house. The cab stood directly below the window, its headlights flared over the front of the house. Felix Racicot saw his son get in the cab. The rear door closed, then the cab went backward down the path. When the cab reached the road, it turned and was lost in the fog and trees and the dark.

Felix Racicot left the window and went to the phone. He took up the receiver. "Jimmy, Byron is gone now. Thank you and Marie for everything.

—Jimmy, could you please put through my call now?

—Ah, it is. Would you please put him on then?"

Felix Racicot waited a moment, then a man's voice came on the line. "Mr. Anza?

—Yes. Felix Racicot here. Sorry to bother you at this hour.

—Ah yes, thank you. It is a pity we haven't met. This business tonight—you did get my message?

—Good. Have you heard from Mr. Lexington?

—Very good. Then the money should be there soon.

—Yes. I'll have a letter of credit drawn up for the rest in the morning. It will probably take most of the day, but you should have the rest by bank closing.

—I know exactly what I'm buying. My son's life. Nothing more, nothing less. Neither I nor my son have the samples nor do we know where they are. To that I can swear.

—Either Mr. Lexington or the girl.

—Good. An hour, then.

—Yes. Thank you very much for your understanding, Mr. Anza."

Felix Racicot put down the receiver. He went to one of the chairs flanking the fireplace and sat. He gazed up at the painting of the man and the woman. He took up a small glass of liqueur and smiled. "Soon."

The driver pulled into the darkened dock and stopped the cab and switched off the motor, as he had been ordered.

Before him, to his left and to his right, as far as he could see, was a forest of masts moving slightly, bobbing, swaying left and right, as the water moved under the boats. Beyond the boats berthed in the docks lay the harbor and the lights and black masses of larger boats anchored there. And beyond the harbor and the anchored boats lay the sea. There the driver saw the red and green lights of a passing freighter. Beyond the sea and the freighter he saw nothing but night.

The driver looked back from the dark harbor to the mirror fixed above the windshield. He saw the heads of two men in the mirror. The men were kissing. One of the men, a boy, made a noise, as if he were trying to pull away from the other man, trying to speak with the other man's mouth on his. Finally the boy pulled away and spoke:

"Lex, no! Listen to me! He's dead. Who killed him?"

The other man laughed and moved away from the boy. "Who *would* kill Ash? I'm the only one I know who would like to kill Ash."

The boy's eyes went forward, not to the mirror, but to something near it, in the front of the cab. The boy's voice was choked. "Get it down. Get it down."

The man leaned forward and placed his hand on the driver's shoulder. "Driver, would it be too much to ask of you to take down the picture of your sweetheart? It upsets my friend."

The driver looked to the sun visor. Clipped there was a newspaper photo of the woman who had been killed at Six Key Cut. Beneath the woman's photo were the block letters

DO YOU
KNOW THIS WOMAN?

The driver reached up and took the newspaper photograph from its clip and laid it on the seat beside him. When

157

he looked back to the mirror, the man was trying to take something from the boy, a case the boy held in his arms, teasing him.

"What have you got there, dear? Something for Lex. May I see?"

The boy struggled with the man. "I'm not trusting you with this. I don't trust you anymore—with anything."

The man released the boy. His voice was light and amused. "You don't? What have I done? I've done everything, haven't I? What haven't I done?"

"You killed Ash," the boy said. "Mehring didn't. They think he did but he didn't. Why did you kill Ash? We can't get out of this without Ash."

The man moved away from the boy. He was no longer amused. "I didn't kill the queer. I can handle these things— let *me* handle this. We're better off without him."

"But he was found in your apartment, Lex. Who did it then? Who?"

The man looked up and met the driver's eyes in the mirror. The man smiled at the driver and his interest in murder and theft and treachery. He turned to the boy. "I don't know. It wasn't me, hon." Now the man spoke thoughtfully. "This doesn't change anything. Even if it is Anza, it could still work in our favor." He looked at the boy. "We'll go ahead with our plan, without Ash. We can do it. I've got a boat, a really nice boat, and a really nice crew. They'll like you, hon. We'll go on exactly as if Ash were here— except we'll take the soap with us now, By. We can have it all. Just you and me."

The boy shrank into the corner. "We've got to give it back."

The man grasped the boy and pulled him to him, pressing the boy's face close to his. "The suds are for Lex, you little pricksucker, and Lex wants his suds now. Now

where have you left . . ." And the man's voice became sound-
less with fury and the driver could only hear scattered words:
". . . where? You fucking idiot . . ."

The man released the boy and struck him, slapping the
boy's face hard to the left, to the right. The boy made no
attempt to hide his face or fend off the blows, his arms still
placed tight around the case. When the man stopped hitting
the boy, the boy fell back, weeping.

". . . no, Lex, don't, I tried it three times this summer.
It worked every time . . ."

Now the man's voice was calm, contemptuous. "Tell
me, how does it work, By?"

"I would leave a package or a case in a locker . . . I
wouldn't put money in it . . . after a day or so they go
through the lockers. They take everything to lost luggage.
They keep it there for thirty days. I would go down and pay
the rent or whatever—ten bucks, and I would have the case
back again."

The man laughed. "Ten million dollars of suds in lost
luggage! By, dear, you have a sense of the bizarre. Have
you ever heard of anything quite so bizarre, driver? A box
of soap worth ten million dollars hidden in lost luggage?"

Both the man and the boy had moved out of the
mirror's frame, so that the driver saw neither of them. He
only heard their voices: "Lex, don't say things like that. He
might know something."

The man laughed. "These people never know anything.
They don't care. You don't care, do you, driver?" The man's
hand touched the driver's shoulder. "Maybe I'll give him a
sample, By, for the little lady. Would the little lady like a
little box of soap worth a quarter million?" The man's hand
went off the driver's shoulder. "They would probably wash
with it—if they washed," said the man and his face came
back into the mirror. He had turned to the boy. "All right.

159

I'll go to the bus station. You stay here. Go to the boat. Count Daddy's money. We're going to need all of it to pay for the boat. I'll go to the bus station and get the case and come back." The man moved across the seat toward the boy. "Is there anything simpler than that, hon?"

"Why can't I go with you? Why do I have to wait here? Don't leave me here. I can go with you to the bus station."

The man spoke impatiently: "Look, there's a boat. There's a crew. I've hired them. They're expecting to be paid *now*. They won't understand that I have to go to the fucking bus station. If they don't have their money, they'll go away and then where will we be? Look, there they are now."

The driver saw something shifting in the dark, a boat moving into the harbor, and behind him came the sound of the rear door being opened. The man had pushed the boy out of the cab. "Lex, wait. How long will you be gone?"

"Only a few minutes. How long is it to the bus station and back, driver? Ten minutes, By, the driver says ten minutes." The door closed. The man spoke to the driver: "Move it, driver. Get the fuck out of here."

The cab pulled away. The boy ran alongside the cab for a few yards, then he stopped. The driver saw the boy in the mirror, standing alone on the dock, his arms wrapped about the case. Then the driver turned the cab and the boy was gone.

Lex went downtown, into the pit of the city. What had maddened the girl smiled on Lex. The freaks and crazies, the bikers and pimps, the dealers and hustlers, the cannibals and killers, Lex went safe among them. Lex was safe downtown because he had done everything. As the cab went

toward downtown he saw the outsiders, the girl or girls like
her and the boys and the tourists and travelers and gawkers
and slummers, those who had made a wrong turn and
couldn't find their way out; those who had seen too much
and those who had not seen enough. Lex could feel their
fear and their desire for him and the freaks and the scum
and the mad, those who had done everything.

Lex left the cab at the bus station. He entered the
bus station, moving like a prince through the freaks and
the fear. Lex was home. He feared nothing now. Felix
Racicot, Mehring from New York, the cops, not even Anza
and the Colombians could touch him here. There was
nothing he couldn't handle. The Racicots he would sell to
the Colombians, Mehring would come foul of the cops or
the Colombians, the cops were so slow and stupid, Lex
would be gone by the time they understood his plan. The
Colombians, in time he would escape them too, in time he
would be working with them again, toying with them, as he
now toyed with the Racicots and Mehring and the cops and
poor Ash, before someone had killed him.

Lex's mood darkened as he crossed the bus-station
hall going toward the baggage room. That was the only
detail not in place—who had killed Ash? But as Lex went
he found nothing in this missing piece to concern him. Someone had done him a favor, that was all. He would have had
to kill Ash himself, sooner or later. He had been robbed of
the pleasure, that was all. In a few moments Lex's plan
would be complete, done but for his own disappearance.
What would it matter if a single *i* had not been dotted? Lex
knew, as he came to the counter where luggage was checked
and retrieved, his plan was perfect, close enough, without it.

An old black man was working the counter. The old
man would not be hurried and he took no one out of turn.

Lex tried to cut in before someone, but the old black man would not serve him. As the old man shuffled here and there, like some turtle in the sand, Lex slapped a coin against the steel counter and laughed at the fools and losers as they came with their stamped plastic valises and boxes tied with string and tattered duffel bags and bright backpacks, all stuffed with rags they called clothes and filthy tennis shoes and caps with earflaps and toys for their moronic children and books like the Bible and How to Succeed in everything under the sun. And there was the garbage from these losers' minds, the ravings they called ideas, letters and strange manifestoes and prayers and sermons and poems and songs, all packed as carefully as treasured illuminated manuscripts in their bags and packs and collapsing suitcases. And there, among all these bundles and bags and cases of junk, was ten million dollars, maybe fifteen, maybe twenty if Lex could hold on to it and sell it pound by pound. Lex could see it there as he stood in line with the fools, the cardboard box sitting high on a back shelf, wrapped in tape, the box printed with words *Snow Drift*, an irony that had driven Lex to choose the box in the first place. Within that box were forty smaller boxes that now each contained eight ounces of uncut cocaine. It was worth more than all the things all these lost souls would ever own.

"Slower! Slower!" Lex cried out as the old black man went here and there, taking tickets, retrieving luggage, matching tickets, giving out the case or bag or box. Lex held the silver dollar between his fingers and beat a tattoo on the metal counter and laughed at the old man till his turn came. The old black man who had been so courteous to others approached Lex:

"Now watch you want, loudmouth?"

Lex smiled at the darkie. "My box of suds, please, there, on the back shelf."

The old man did not turn where Lex had indicated. "You gots your ticket?"

"Ticket? No. No ticket, fool. It's mine. I can see it. I can identify it. A box of soap samples. *Look*."

"You gots to have your ticket. Any fool can come up and point to some box on a shelf and say it his. We don't run no carnival booth here. You gots to have your ticket."

Lex laughed. "Now wait, I suppose I haven't made myself understood. I'm no bus rider. I didn't check this box on a fucking bus. So I don't have a fucking ticket. I left the case in a locker there—over there—and I became involved in business affairs and I forgot to put an extra quarter in the locker. And so they came and took the box away. And so I've come to claim it and pay whatever rental I owe. How much simpler can I make it?"

The old man ignored the coin. He turned and looked back toward the shelves of suitcases and boxes and bags. "You're right there. That is the shelf where we puts things that are left overtime in the lockers." The old man turned back to Lex. He pushed the silver dollar away. "This won't buy you nothing. That will be ten dollars."

"Ten bucks? All right, all right. Ten fucking bucks."

"It happen to people who tries to cheats on their locker." As Lex took a bill from his wallet, the old man reached under the counter and brought out a printed form. "And you gots to fill out this form."

"What the fuck for? I'm paying you ten bucks and I'm telling you what's mine and I want it!"

The old man placed a square black finger on the form. "We needs your name and present address and here you puts the contents of your parcel and here you sign your name. And you gots to have ID."

Lex opened his wallet and flung his driver's license on the counter. "All right. All right. Name, address, signature.

Contents: forty boxes of soap." Lex tore at the form with his pen. The old man took the paper and studied every line carefully. "Hurry up! Christ!"

In time the old man nodded. "That seem right." He put the form and Lex's license and the ten-dollar bill on the counter. "Now we gots to have the key."

"Key? What key?"

The old man placed his black finger on the form. "We gots to have the old key to the locker. That's in the regulations."

Lex leaned back, laughing, his body arched. He came forward. "The key, you old turkey, I put the key in the locker! It's there. Here, let me explain to you. I walk up, put the key in the locker, turn the key, click, door opens, box gone, key remains in lock. Got it?"

"You remember the number of your locker?"

"Remember the number—I don't have to remember any fucking number! That's my box and I fucking want it!"

The old man shook his head. He reached under the counter. "You ain't got a key, you can't remember the number, then you got to fill out this form. You write down what's your property and what's in it. We call in the police and open it. They agree, you pay the ten bucks, it's yours."

Lex struck his forehead. "Oh damn! Now I remember! I lost it. That's why I don't have my key. I lost the mother-fucker."

The old man reached under the counter. "For lost keys you have to fill out another form." He placed another form on the counter. "And you is going to have to come back in the morning to talk to Mr. Robertson. I is just the night clerk and unauthorized to deal with lost keys. That is done during the day."

Lex reached across the counter and grasped the old man's arm. "Wait. Listen. I can't wait till morning. I've got to have those samples now. I'm a salesman. Soap salesman. Look, I'll pay you for the case. A hundred bucks. Forget the key, the forms, everything. Okay? A hundred bucks."

The old man looked at Lex's hand on his shirt sleeve. He removed his arm. "You tell me you a soap salesman and you gots to sell soap in the middle of the night and gots to sell it so bad you going to pay a hundred bucks for soap you can gets in the grocery store for twenty dollars?"

Lex snatched the form from the counter. "All right. I'll wait. I'll come back in the morning. I'll fill out the form. I'll find the key. I'll talk to the chief—what's his name?"

"Mr. Robertson," said the old man. "You can come back and talk to him. I advise that."

Lex sneered. "Robertson—is he a nigger too?"

The old black man shook his head. "No. He a honkie."

Lex went back across the bus-station hall. Now even the crazies and freaks stepped out of his way. He went screaming at the top of his lungs: "Fuckingniggermother-fuckingsonofabitch I'll kill him I'll kill every fucking niggermotherfuckingniggersniggersniggers I'll kill all you fucking niggers out of my fucking way!"

A large black man in an army master sergeant's uniform looked balefully across the hall at Lex and Lex changed his course and went out the bus station's main exit. Out in the night Lex's rage became a howl of derision. He put his head back and laughed, mad. Then he turned and walked up the street, jabbering as wildly as any walkie-talkie in the city. "It's perfect. Fucking perfect! It's like fate! It's like revenge!" Tourists skittered out of the way. Travelers held their luggage tight. People left the sidewalk, they hugged the wall, as Lex went along. "For years I've been trying to get rid of that little cunt Jamie! And now she's got the key to ten million fucking dollars!"

Lex came to the end of the widewalk. He stood at an

alleyway and thought it out. The girl had the key. All right. By had given her the key at the motel. She had left the motel and come to the bus station. The locker was empty. She had gone back to the motel. By was gone. She left the motel. She went to her apartment. By wasn't there either. She couldn't stay there, the place was hot. She went looking for the boy. She went to Lex's place. Cops everywhere. Wrapping up Ash. The girl would flee. To the streets. Where would she go from the streets? Lex smiled. Of course. So simple. So obvious. She would go to Daddy's. That's where the boy would be. He had been there only minutes ago. She would be there now. Probably just arriving with the key to ten million dollars in her pocket. Lex could catch a cab and be there just in time.

As if his thoughts had been read, a cab's lights flashed on down the alley and came toward Lex from the dark. Lex raised his hand to call out to the cab, but as the cab came out of the shadows the driver spoke to him.

"Lex," he said.

FIFTEEN

JAMIE saw the tear in the fence and went through it. She came into a wall of stinging nettles and she went through them. There the earth gave way beneath her and she was flung into space. She struck something hard as she went down. She struck the ragged wall again and again till she was rolling along its slanted plane. Then she struck a bed of sand, soft and moist, and she rolled on her back and did not move till her breath came back to her, soothed by the water and soft sand.

Jamie came to her knees. Two high, tilted walls enclosed her. She had fallen into the viaduct that ran through the city. Panic took hold of Jamie—she was trapped in this winding prison, with no escape but into the swamp or to the sea—but then she remembered having seen the viaduct from above, from the freeway overpass that turned into the airport. Jamie came to her feet. The viaduct wasn't a trap. It was a haven. She was safe here, from the freaks and the Colombians and the cops and everyone who wanted her. Jamie turned and began walking along the sand, skirting the shallow pools of water. It was more than a haven, it was a highway all her own that would lead her to the airport.

Jamie walked a half hour, till the sky took on a dull orange cast, the glow from the lights of the airport terminal and the maintenance hangars and the parking lots that surrounded the hangars and the terminal. Beyond she could hear the jets working up their engines for takeoff and the pop and squeal of the tires of the jets touching down and the hushed roar of their engines being reversed. Jamie went to the wall and put her hands on it, digging her fingers and the toes of her shoes into the ragged surface that had ripped her flesh and clothes in falling. She went up the wall in one quick climbing run.

The kids who worked for the man who ran the car-rental parking lot called him Papa. Because of his great silver beard, Papa figured, and he was so good to these kids, maybe that was some of it too. These kids, hippies, pill-poppers, dopers, just plain brats, smoking their weeds, bopping around with ghetto blasters in their ears, pushing Papa's nice shiny sedans around like they were beach buggies or stocks from Daytona Beach—even then Papa treated them as if they were his own. And banging up the cars and leaving roaches in the ashtrays and telling customers to fuck off, that was the least of it. Papa could live with that. What was the hard part was finding these little bastards and when you found them making them work. Well, tonight was going to be the end of it, Papa decided when he saw the kid trying to bug out behind the cars back in the farthest, darkest corner of the rent-a-car lot. Tonight Papa was going to see one of these junior opium eaters put in a good night's work.

Papa picked up his clipboard and went after the kid. But when he had finally tracked her down, cowering there in the back corner of the lot, crouched behind the El Dorado like some kind of small hunted animal, her face stone white with fear, when Papa saw the girl up close, he lost heart. The girl looked so lost and unhappy, looking like she was twelve years old in her baggy clothes, that Papa didn't have much fire in it when he dragged the girl from the car. He chewed her ass for trying to bug out and made her put on the rent-a-car yellow coveralls and put her to work pushing cars from the airport to the lot, probably the first time the kid had worked in her life, Papa told himself, but still he didn't feel too good about working the girl who should have a home with her own mama and papa.

Papa took a liking to the kid the thirty minutes or so she worked before she split. She was a good driver, quick and neat, she didn't smoke reefers, not in the cars anyway, and she hustled cars hard, for the time she worked. But then after the third or fourth car, the girl was gone. Papa waited, cussing the kids of this generation, but his heart wasn't in it. He missed the kid. Papa wished he had given the kid her ten bucks right away. So she would have had a couple bucks when she got back downtown. The way the girl had looked so small and alone when Papa had come up on her, she was going to need every nickel she could lay her hands on to survive that jungle. But after the third or fourth car, the kid was gone and she never came back.

Margot would have recognized Jamie anyway, she thought, without the sign, standing there looking like a frightened clown in the bright yellow jumpsuit. Margot

169

came on the girl in the Eastern concourse, half crouched between a phone shell and soft-drink machine, with Margot's name hand-lettered in lipstick on a piece of paper, the *t* dropped. Margot took the girl under her arm and led her down the concourse, the girl's head tucked against Margot's shoulder. When they reached the end of the concourse the girl had done with her cry. Margot turned the girl toward the car-rental kiosk, but the girl would not follow her. She pulled away from Margot.

"I can't go there," the girl said. "Not there."

"Why not, hon?" said Margot.

The girl looked all about her. "I've just stolen one of their cars."

"I see," said Margot. "Well then, shall we take a taxi?"

"No, no," said the girl. "Not there. I can't go anywhere. Don't you see? Don't you see them? They're everywhere. They're covering every exit. We're trapped."

The two women had come to the terminal's main hall, airline baggage and ticket counters stretching to the ends of the long hall, car-rental desks here, a bar and coffee and gift shop there, before them the glass facade of the terminal main floor.

"Who exactly is it, hon, who is everywhere?"

"The Colombians," said the girl. "They are everywhere. Look. There's one now."

Margot saw a small dark man in a glossy suit, but he seemed to be bustling about his own business, with no interest in either of the women.

"Ah well," said Margot, taking the girl under her arm again. "Let's freshen up then. To the powder room."

Once in the women's room the girl wept again. A confession poured from her that Margot only partially understood. ". . . we're not murderers—we didn't mean to kill them. By told me he knew a med student—he would get them . . . *them* from the hospital. Oh my God, it's so horrible—I didn't know it was Mr. Goodge and the woman—please, please believe me. I didn't know she was alive. I didn't know . . ."

Margot let the girl go on till she was quiet in her arms. She was so small that Margot felt for the time she comforted her that Jamie was still a child, the girl she had seen in the photographs and snapshots Sid had received. Margot led the girl to the basin and washed her face. They then went to the back of the women's room and Margot put Jamie into the last stall, sitting her on the toilet seat. Margot knelt before the girl. "Now we have to begin somewhere, hon. Where is By?"

The girl shook her head. "Dead. He must be by now. He was at the motel. And I left. And I went back. He was gone. He wouldn't leave me. They must have come and taken him away. They've killed him by now. I know it."

"I see. Have you seen Sidney, hon?"

The girl turned her face to the stall partition. "He's dead. He was in the room across the street. I wasn't supposed to go home. But I didn't have any money. The locker was empty. I didn't have a quarter. I didn't know what to do. I saw the man across the street. It was Captain Mehring. But I didn't know him. Then Lex came up behind him and hit him. I saw the body. I think he's dead. I don't know . . ."

"I see. Well, I think we can worry about Sidney later. He has a habit of seeming dead at times and then turning up quite alive." Margot raised the girl's head. The girl's eyes were glazed, near shock. "I really don't enjoy doing this, hon, but you really must snap out of it. You won't feel a thing." Margot slapped the girl twice. Something flared in the girl's eyes and Margot pulled the girl to her feet and

171

shook her till the girl's body stiffened and she could stand on her own. Then Margot sat the girl on the toilet seat and stroked her hair. "There. Now don't you feel much better?"

"No," said the girl and she and Margot laughed. They embraced and the girl cried briefly.

"Now hon," said Margot, "I think really we must go to the police."

"Police? No, Margot, please. I know, I know! I'll have to go sooner or later, but can we find By first? Please! I want to be with him. Then we'll go—together."

"Then By isn't dead."

The girl lowered her head. "No. He left me."

"Well, we must take a first step." Margot rose and the girl stood with her. "Let's go to Sidney's hotel. If he's dead the room will be free and we can have a bath and lie down and I'll make some phone calls and we'll find By."

The girl shook her head. "What about the Colombians?"

"Are there really any Colombians, hon? Perhaps you were just imagining things."

"Maybe . . . maybe I was. It's all—everything's been so crazy tonight. Maybe they weren't there at all."

"There's a good girl," said Margot. "Let's take a look."

The two women went the length of the long rest room, empty but for someone in one of the stalls.

Margot stopped the girl before the door. "Now remember, hon, not all small dark men are Colombians."

The girl smiled weakly. "Okay."

The two women went from the women's room. Once in the hall they stopped immediately. Three large dark men stood in the hall. One placed to the left, one to the right and one directly across from the women's-room door. There was another large dark man speaking on a telephone farther down the hall. The three nearby men came toward the two women.

"Colombians," said Margot, and she and the girl went back into the women's room.

Margot and Jamie went toward the end of the women's room, to the last stall where they had been. The woman who had occupied the other stall had come out now and stood before one of the basins. The woman was a stewardess, pretty, but no longer young. She was crying angrily over the sink. Margot spoke to the stewardess.

"Are you in trouble, hon?"

"Fucking bastard," said the stewardess.

"Yes. We—my friend and I are in trouble. Could you possibly call the police when you leave and have them come here?"

"No! No!" cried the girl. "Margot, you promised! No police!"

The stewardess dried her face. "Well, do you want me to call the cops or not?"

Margot looked at the girl, so frail and frightened. "I guess not."

"What's the trouble?" said the stewardess.

"Boyfriend."

"Oh *that*," said the stewardess and looked her face over in the mirror and left the women's room.

Margot and the girl went to the end of the women's room and entered the last stall. Margot looked about the cubicle. "Well, we're safe here for a while, I suppose, but sooner or later, hon, they're going to come in for us."

The girl looked around. "Is there a window?"

"No window." Margot fingered the collar of the bright yellow jump suit. "I could put on this dreadful thing and change my hair and make a run for it. It might draw them away from the door long enough for you to escape."

The girl shook her head. "Margot, you are so *big*."

"I am rather tall," said Margot. "Well, I do know a bit of karate. We might cause enough of a disturbance to attract the security forces or whatever they have around here."

"They'll just squash us like bugs. I've seen them do it."

A sound came from the entrance of the women's room. The outer door opened, then the inner door. There was the hiss of its closing. Margot pushed the stall door to and closed the lock, without making a sound. There was silence, then heavy footfalls, then the sound of the most distant stall door being opened, then more footfalls and the second stall door being opened, all accompanied by some muttered and labored breathing. Margot bent down and looked under the stall partition. She saw a pair of men's work boots and legs in khaki trousers moving the length of the women's room, the broad flat boots pounding the floor, the stall doors being thrown back, one by one.

Margot straightened. The girl's eyes were wide with fear. Margot placed her hand over the girl's mouth and pushed her into the corner of the stall. Margot rolled her skirt to her waist, baring her good legs. Slam, thud, thud, slam, thud, thud, came the sounds of the intruder approaching the last stall in line. Margot carefully lifted the stall door latch, bent her knees and flexed her arms and legs and assumed an attack position.

The slapping feet and slamming stall doors came closer till the khaki trouser legs and broad worker's boots stood before the last stall. "Heh heh heh," said the intruder.

With that Margot kicked the stall door, slamming it into the intruder. Margot came flashing out of the stall. She whipped a second kick at the intruder's ample midriff, slammed a fat round nose with an extended knuckle and cracked a shin, while giving out her sorority warning cry: "Man on the floor! Man on the floor!"

The burly figure in the lumberjack shirt reeled back from Margot's attack, slammed against the sink and fell to the floor, growling and holding her nose. "I ain't no goddamn man," said the intruder.

Margot looked at the stocky figure dressed like a lumberjack. "Oh dear, you aren't, are you?"

"Bet your boots," said the mannish woman.

"Oh my dear, I've hurt you," said Margot and bent over the woman, who grinned at Margot's good legs.

"Not much."

Margot lowered her skirt and helped the lady lumberjack to her feet. She washed her face and tended her swollen nose and explained the problem to the lady lumberjack.

"Now there are three, maybe four, very large dangerous men lurking about outside the women's room. They are trying to abduct my friend Jamie here and we need some help. Did you see them when you came in?"

"Nah. But I wasn't looking," said the lady lumberjack, who was called Duffy. "I don't see the problem. I can take two of them. You got a good kick, sister, you take one—did you say there was three or four?"

"We must plan as if there are four. Two for you, one for me—we'll need another hand if Jamie is going to escape."

"Right," said Duffy. "We'll draft the next sister who comes through the door."

There came the sound of the outer door opening and closing and a gaunt figure entered the women's room. The woman was between forty and fifty, tall, thin, ethereal, with the distracted air of a small-town librarian. Her hair was done back in a strict bun. She wore a seasoned tweed suit,

175

wire-rimmed glasses and sensible shoes. Her face was pale and ascetic, her look bemused. She approached the three women in an otherwordly fashion. "Hello there," she said with a smile.

"Christ," said the lady lumberjack.

"I don't think we have time to wait for a replacement," said Margot, looking the librarian up and down. "My dear, we're having a bit of a problem tonight."

"Hooligans?" said the woman and reached back to her bun and withdrew a hairpin which she moved around like a fencer waggling his foil.

"Better," said Duffy as the librarian's hair fell to her shoulders.

"You will do fine," said Margot, taking the woman's frail arm and placing her to one side of Jamie. The lady lumberjack stood on the other. "Did you see the four Latin gentlemen lurking in the hall as you came in?"

"Yes. Villains."

"They are indeed. They have come for our friend Jamie here and we must see that she escapes them—even if it means some sacrifice on our part."

"We shall take them," said the librarian.

"Good," said Margot. "Now I think it would be best if we formed ourselves around Jamie—Duffy on the right— what is your name, dear?"

"Margaret," said the librarian.

"Margaret on the left and I will take the point."

"A phalanx," said the librarian.

"Say what?" said Duffy.

"A flying wedge," said Margot.

"Better," said Duffy.

"We will leave the women's room together, in formation. Duffy will take the man to the right, Margaret the man to the left, and I will occupy the man blocking our way. If our attack is coordinated, Jamie should be able to escape in the confusion." Margot placed herself at the head of the small formation. "Are we ready?"

"I'm prepared."

"Can't wait."

"This will never work," said the girl.

"Nonsense," Margot said. "Now Jamie, when we strike you must run like the wind. Now, girls—go!" said Margot and led the closed-formed quartet out of the women's room into the hall.

The thugs grinned at the sight of the women. The leader approached the group, chewing a matchstick. "Okay, girls. Let's break it up."

"Hai ya!" cried out Margot and aimed a flying kick at the thug. The thug caught Margot's heel and flipped her in the air. Margot landed on her backside, her good legs showing.

Duffy doubled her fists and Margaret waggled her hairpin. The thug just grinned. His associates approached.

SIXTEEN

THREE cars—Anza's limousine and two large late-model sedans—were parked forming a triangle in the warehouse. The cars' doors were open to the interior of the triangle they made. There six or so large dark men in suits stood about, facing the limousine. The warehouse was empty but for a few crates and machines—a forklift and a small crane —set against the back wall. The warehouse was dark but for the interior lights of the cars. Near the cars was a small shed or office whose door was locked and guarded by two more men in suits. From time to time muffled cries came from the boy being held in the shed. Anza, the Colombian maestro, sat in the back of the limousine, speaking on the limo phone to an associate in New York.

"Ah, Rupert, the irony of it," said Anza. "Do you say that neither plane carried the load? All my exercise for nothing. Who would have thought Swede had the brains for such a maneuver? But then why would they have used these children—am I correct?

—Ah yes, Swede was so talented. But we must understand that sooner or later even good men succumb to temptation. It is the nature of our commerce, I think. So much value so condensed. Who among us would not be tempted to put ten million in a suitcase and walk away?"

There came a sound from outside the warehouse—a tap on a car horn—and the men standing about the cars became alert. The car horn came again, two quick notes, and one of the men spoke to another in Spanish. That man went toward a large corrugated door at the front of the warehouse. He opened a box by the door and pressed a switch and the door rolled back, revealing a large late-model car like the others. The car's lights went off and it pulled into the warehouse. The door closed behind it. The car went to the small shed and stopped. Four men got out of the car, the two coming from the backseat bringing two women with them. One of the sentinels at the door of the shed unfastened the lock. When he opened the door the boy within the shed tried to come out, but the sentinels pushed the boy back. The two women were put in the shed and the door was locked again and the sentinels took up their position.

Anza made no acknowledgment of the arrival of the car and the two women but to pull the car door closed. He spoke on the phone: "No, that won't be a problem. It seems we've struck a preemptive blow.

—Yes. Mike too, I'm afraid. When the stakes run this high, laxity and treachery become the same.

—Are you saying, then, the shipment never left Barranquilla?

—That's no good, Rupert. We must find it then. But

then such things are easier to locate at home. There is really nowhere to hide there."

The men talked a few minutes more, then came the sound of another car horn, played lightly, from outside the warehouse. Anza turned in his seat to watch the man opening the warehouse door. Outside the door sat another car. It did not come into the warehouse. Anza turned and signaled one of the men who stood away from the others, the slender youth named Marcel. Marcel went to the shed. He unlocked the door and opened it. The two guards and Marcel went into the shed and pulled the boy out the door. The boy was weeping, begging for his life, as they brought him across the warehouse. The two guards dragged the boy to the open door and the car waiting there. The guards put the boy in the waiting car and stood inside the door as it rolled down. Anza waited till the door lowered. He then turned back to the phone:

"Felix has just come for him now.

—Oh yes, the boy's quite all right. A bit frightened, but a little fright might do him good. A cheap lesson. Rupert, if it weren't for my great admiration for you, the lesson would have been much, much dearer.

—Rupert, I am not a brigand. We don't deal with men like Felix Racicot like that. His son is as safe as my own.

—Of course I understand these old loyalties. We have them in my country as well. How else can men such as we operate—if not as gentlemen?"

Marcel had returned to the limousine. Anza opened the door and motioned Marcel to come into the back. Anza smiled at Marcel and took a long thin cigar from his pocket and handed it to the youth. The youth clipped the end from the cigar and gave it back to Anza. Marcel took a lighter from his pocket and lit the cigar for Anza. Anza smiled as he smoked and spoke to his associate on the phone:

"Ah, how I wish I could be there, Rupert, but I must sail this morning.

—I think we must have some settlement this week. Shall we say—day after tomorrow?

—Yes. We have some cash already. The boy had it with him. But I'm afraid it's not nearly enough.

—Ah, that figure will do. You must understand, Rupert, that my concern is not so much the cash involved— though of course there is always that—but that my reputation be maintained. One simply cannot be made a fool of in this business and survive.

—Of course.

—Yes. Yes.

—Oh well, thank you, Rupert. And a very good night to you."

Anza handed the phone to Marcel, who replaced it in its cradle. Anza studied the cigar in his hand, then threw back his head: "Old school ties." Then he spoke to Marcel in Spanish: "Racicot and Rupert have taken the cocaine. What fools do these gentlemen think we are? They say it has never left Colombia." Anza studied the smoke curling from the cigar. He moved his hand through it, like a sculptor working a figure. "Kill Racicot. The boy as well. In their house, as if it were a burglary. I will be sailing at dawn. Wait till then."

"And Rupert?"

"In a month's time I shall lunch with Rupert in his club in New York. By then he will have learned his lesson."

Marcel looked toward the shed. "And the women?"

Anza smiled. "We have no need for them. They have become merely unfortunately involved. We may not be gentlemen, Marcel, but let them live."

Marcel got out of the car. He spoke to one of the men, who went to the front of the warehouse and pressed the switch that operated the door. The door rose and the men went to the cars and the cars' motors were started and the cars went out of the warehouse, the smaller cars following the limousine.

Margot and Jamie had come to the warehouse in the back of a large late-model car, placed tightly between two large dark men. The car went from the bright and noise of the airport to a dark, deserted part of the city. The women were told to close their eyes and lower their heads, and they did so, obediently. At one point, when she heard a sound outside the car, Margot had opened her eyes, but the man by her pushed her head to her knees and Margot did not open her eyes again. They drove for ten, fifteen minutes, the car making many turns, stopping briefly now and then. At length the car stopped a final time and the men said the women could raise their heads and open their eyes.

Margot saw a corrugated iron door in the headlights. The driver tapped the horn and there came the whine of an electric motor behind the door and the door raised. When the door had risen, the car pulled into the gloom and went deep into the warehouse. Margot saw other cars there in the warehouse, three of them, pulled into a triangle, their doors open, their interior lights on, their windows lit like jack-o'-lanterns. The car pulled to a stop before a small cubicle, a shed or an office of some kind, in the rear of the warehouse. The men who had pinioned the women got out of the car, each taking one of the women with him. Margot saw that one of the circled cars was a limousine, but she did not turn her head to see more. Two men stood by the shed door. One of them slid back a bolt on the door. When the bolt was withdrawn the door flew open and a boy within the shed lunged at the door, trying to run out. One of the men struck the boy and the boy cried out and staggered backward, into the shed. The women were pushed into the shed. They heard the bolt closing behind them.

The women stood inside the door. The boy cowered against the far wall. The girl cried out the boy's name, but there was no recognition in his eyes, only fear. When the girl ran to him and flung her arms around him, he threw her aside, his eyes on Margot, who had stayed by the door. The girl went to the boy again and he did not push her away. She caressed him and kissed him, but he did not seem to notice.

"Oh By, By, By, when you disappeared I thought you were dead. I thought they had come and taken you . . ."

The boy's look went from Margot to the girl to the door. His eyes jerked here and there, he could not keep them still. "Dead! I *am* dead. We all are dead. Don't you understand that, you bitch? I am dead. You, you fucking bitch, you have killed me."

"No, no! We're alive. They don't want us! They want the cocaine, that's all they want. They don't care about us."

The corners of the boy's mouth twisted back. His look came back to Margot. "Who is that?"

The boy held the girl's hands now. He twisted them, but she did not pull away. "By, don't!—she's a friend. She knows Sid Mehring. She's come from New York."

"Mehring? Mehring?"

"By, there was no one else to turn to. I thought you were dead!"

The boy released the girl and slapped her. Margot went toward the couple and the boy shrank away from the women. "Stay away from me, you fucking whores! Both of you!" Margot drew near and held the girl. "Don't you understand? She's one of Mehring's spies. He's been plotting against me from the start. Lex was right. He's a killer." The boy turned his fury to Margot. "Killer! Killer!"

The girl tried to go to the boy, but Margot would not release her. "By, no—she's trying to help us."

"*Help* us!" The boy laughed. "Did you know Mehring's killed Ash? He murdered Ash!"

The boy took to the floor, curling into a ball, weeping. Margot released the girl and the girl went to the boy. He accepted her comfort like a child. Margot stood away from the pair.

"What I wouldn't give for a cigarette. Jamie, hon, these men, are they as dangerous as they seem?"

The boy raised. "Dangerous! They're killers! They're going to kill us all, you stupid cunt!"

"Yes. Well. What would induce them *not* to kill us? What if you gave back this drug you've taken from them? Would that help?"

The boy freed himself from the girl and stood. He had grown calm. But this calm, Margot thought, disfigured him more than had his cowardice. The boy walked back and forth, thinking as he went. "It would help, it would . . . but we don't have it. Lex has taken it." The boy went to the girl. He knelt and touched her face. "Lex has betrayed me, baby. Don't you see? Lex, it was Lex—he started it all." The boy stood. "Lex killed Goodge. He did." He spoke to Margot now, control gathering in him like decay. "That's what started it all. Goodge, he was blackmailing Lex about the letters. Lex wrote the letters."

The girl turned her face from the boy, so that she would not have to watch him lie.

"The Eat the Rich letters?" said Margot.

The boy looked about the room. "Those. And he wrote the other letters too. The ones from Mehring. The ones the cops found in Jamie's apartment."

The girl turned to the boy. "What letters from Mehring?"

The boy laughed. "The ones from Mehring—how the two of you fucked. He knows how you fucked Mehring, baby, he saw it every night from the Room."

The girl shrank against the wall. "The room?"

The boy sneered. "The Room across from your apartment. It was you and Lex. You two. Lex and you, everything was your idea. I had nothing to do with it. The letters, the blackmail, the burn, the Six Key crash—everything! The two of you did it all! *You* killed Goodge and the woman. The woman at Six Key, she was yours too!"

The girl lowered her head. "No, no," she said.

Margot turned from the girl, with the first thing on her mind a good kick for the boy, when she saw the boy had stopped. He stood motionless, listening. Now Margot heard the sounds from beyond the shed, the whine of the electrical motor, the crank of the door as it rose.

A smile lit the boy's face. He held a finger to his lips. "They're leaving," he whispered.

But there was no sound from the cars and then they heard footsteps approaching the door and the bolt being slid back. The door opened and two men came into the room. The boy fell to his knees. He was weeping now, his hands clasped and raised. The men took the boy's hands and broke them apart and lifted him to his feet and dragged him from the shed. The boy screamed as he was being dragged away, but his words meant nothing now. The men dragged the boy from the shed, past the limousine and the other cars. They dragged him to the warehouse door where a car stood, waiting, its headlights flashing over the boy and the men. The men dragged the boy to the waiting car and put him in the car and closed the door. The boy huddled on the floorboard. "It's in the soapbox! It's in the soap! It's at the bus station! The lockers! It's in the lockers!" the boy cried out. The warehouse door closed on the car and the man at the

185

wheel raised his clenched fists high over the weeping boy's head, but when he brought his hands down he held the boy's head, gently, till his crying ceased. It was all Felix Racicot could do now. It was too late for anything else.

The door closed and the two women waited. They stood together against the far wall waiting for the men to come for them, but they did not come. They heard the whine and the clanking of the warehouse door being lowered and then a short time later the sounds of the door being raised. They heard the cars being started, one after another, and then the squeal of tires as the cars turned and went away. Then there was silence.

Margot waited, then went to the door. She stood, listening. She heard nothing. She turned the knob and pushed the door open. She stepped from the shed. The warehouse was empty. The door at the far end stood open. She returned to the shed and took Jamie and led her from the room, across the warehouse and out the door into the night.

The women walked quickly down a long deserted street. On one side of the street was a high wire fence and beyond railroad tracks, on the other stood a wall of warehouses like the one they had left. They kept on the street, walking in the shadows of the warehouses, stopping in doorways when they heard a distant sound. But the men had gone. They were free.

Margot saw the phone box at the end of the street—a lighted glass box glowing in the dark. Margot took Jamie by the arm and they ran toward the phone box.

Margot turned to the girl. "We've got to call now, Jamie. We can't wait. It's too late."

The girl pleaded with her: "No, no, please, not the police. Please don't call the police. Not yet."

Margot closed her eyes. "All right. I'll call a cab. We'll go to Sidney's hotel. *Then* we'll call the police."

The girl nodded. "Yes. Then we'll call the police."

Margot went into the phone box. She took a dime, lifted the receiver and put the coin in the slot. She thought back to the numbers, numbers she remembered without trying, numbers she remembered when she wanted to forget them. The Miami cop who had called Sid in New York, she couldn't remember his name, but his number was still there. Three, four in the morning, she would call him anyway. There would be a referral, a switchboard, something. "Sorry, Jamie," Margot said and turned the dial.

A soft voice came on the line. "Yes?"

"Are you the officer who called Sid Mehring in New York? About the accident at Six Key?"

"Yes."

"I have Jamie Simmons with me—the missing girl. She wants to turn herself in."

"Where are you?"

"Oh, I don't know. Wait. There's an address on the phone." Margot gave the man the street number and there was a pause, then the man repeated the address. "Yes. That's it. Can you come quickly? Please."

"I'll be there right away," said the soft voice. "You were right to call." And the connection was broken.

SEVENTEEN

THE Firefly was closed now. It was late and the doors had been shut. There was a body or two strewn about the bar floor, but Thelma had a soft spot for a sleeping wino and she let them snooze away. Let the swamper move the poor devils around so he could sweep. Thelma didn't care if the winos were still there curled around a barstool for the morning shift, she was such a touch when it came to letting people without hope have a rest.

The two cops, Berger and Daniels, had come in just before closing time, just as Thelma was pitching out the last walking drunk, they were on their own, and closing the doors. Thelma liked cops, these cops, the big guys, Berger and Daniels. They had helped her out of a couple of scrapes before, and she bought them a beer. But the cops didn't drink much. They had come on business, the business that had been bothering Thelma. It was why she had called.

The big cop, the really big cop, Berger, pulled out the woman's photograph, the picture that had been in all the papers. Except that this was the original, a glossy of the woman who had been killed at Six Key. The dead woman didn't look too good in this big, clear photo. She hadn't looked so dead in the newspaper photo. Newspaper photos did that, Thelma thought, they didn't make things look as good or as bad as they really were, in the original.

Thelma looked over the photo and pushed it back to the cops. "Yeah, that's her. Wino Wanda. Don't know her real name. That's what we called her."

"And she was in here last night?"

"That's right. She was with a guy. Last night, whatever night it was. I got a notion it was the guy who killed her."

"Tell us about him, Thelma."

"Well, he was a drunk, you know, they both were. I'd seen them—him and the woman—around for a couple weeks, drinking and fighting. Holding hands and banging around. They were like all these wino couples. Always up or down. Fucking or fighting. Nothing in between."

"Like some people we know, right, Thelma?"

"Speak for yourself, Dan. Me and Paulie got a good relationship."

The cop laughed. "You remember anything else about this guy?"

"Yeah, well, he was a wino, like all the rest of them, but he was different, this guy, somehow. You know how all these winos are full of beans? You know, Mal, they are all the lost son of King Ranch, they have been disinherited for marrying a spic or lost it in a booray game or they are CIA agents. You know, they jump out of airplines, or they are

189

war heroes. You ought to hear the battles they seen—Guadal-canal, Dien Bien Phu, you name it, they been there and they have killed enough gooks China is empty."

The cops laughed. "So this guy wasn't the war-hero type?"

"Well, you see, I think maybe he was. He never said nothing about the war, but there was something about him, kinda the way he stood up straight. The way he moved around, even when he was drunk. He had this, whattaya call it? Military bearing. And he was neat and he was polite, when he was sober, but it was the look in his eye, like maybe he really had done all these things the other winos just blow about. And the way he talked, like he come from some kinda good family, not the King Ranch maybe, but he talked, when he talked, he didn't talk that much, but when he did talk, he talked good. Like he'd had some kinda education. Military school maybe."

"Give you much trouble?"

"Nah. He wasn't a bad drunk. He just had this look about him, like he meant business. He did punch one guy out one night. This guy, some tourist who couldn't hold his booze, he was messing with Wanda, his lady friend, and this guy clipped him. It wasn't that big a deal. Nobody hardly noticed it. One minute the guy was tonguing Wanda and the next minute the guy was sitting down in the corner. I didn't even boot him out."

"Did you ever see him choke or strangle anybody, or try to?"

"Well, not choke or strangle anybody, but one night some of the winos were horsing around, you know, showing their karate kicks and judo throws and boxing punches, and there was this big guy, he bet Wanda's friend he couldn't take him down. This guy, he reaches up and takes the big guy's collar at the sides, like this, and then he gives a little flick with his wrists and the big guy was out like a light. Standing there on his feet. The other guy, he caught the big guy and sat him on a barstool. In a minute, half a minute maybe, the guy was back, swigging his beer. I don't think he ever knew he had been out."

"Anything else you remember about the guy that might help us identify him? We'd really like to talk to him."

"Let's see. They called him some nickname. Like some boxer, you know. Lefty or Slugger or Rocky. Something like that."

Berger put a ten-dollar bill on the counter. "You say this guy was in here again? Tonight?"

"That's right," said Thelma, taking up the bill and smoothing the wrinkles out of it. Cops were always carrying money wadded up in their pockets, like little kids, so their coins wouldn't jingle. "That's why I called. He was in here last night. Tonight, I mean. This shift."

"Tell us about it, Thelma."

"Well, he was different. I didn't recognize him at first. Not till later, when I got to thinking about it."

"How was he different, Thelma?"

"He was sober. All cleaned up. Neat as a pin. But it was more than that. I seen winos come and go. I seen them down and dirty. I seen them on the up and up." Thelma gave her arm a rub, as if the doors were still open and a cool breeze had come through the bar. "But this guy, he looked like he meant business. It was in his eyes."

"Tell us everything he did and said, Thelma. Don't leave anything out. We really do want to talk to this guy."

"Well, he was sitting there, on the end barstool. It was quiet. About six, before the action starts. He was here when the story about Wanda came on the TV. I was standing there, watching it. He was right behind me."

"How did he react when he saw the story?"

191

"That I don't know. I had my back to him. I couldn't tell. See, he asked about Wanda when he first came in. Not by name. He just asked. And I didn't make the connection. I just wasn't thinking. I was watching the TV."

"Anything else, Thelma? Anything."

"He wanted to see a phone book. I gave it to him. I thought he was a screwball, all this good mystery on the TV and him sitting there reading the phone book."

"He was looking for a number?"

"Yeah. He had this napkin with him, maybe a piece of paper. He had this word written on it. One word. It was like Latin. You know, these guys come in here writing shit on the napkins all the time. All sorts of weird stuff—algebra and foreign languages and things from the Bible and little diagrams for inventions that don't mean shit. Well, this guy had this word in Latin. The word for king, you know, like a dog's name. Rex. Like the guy who bangs his mama and they poke his eyes out. You seen the movie."

"It couldn't have been Lex?"

"What? Nah. I used to have a boyfriend, that's what we called him. Eatapussy Rex."

It was one of Thelma's good ones, but the cops didn't laugh. They acted like they didn't get it at all. "Think about it. Lex—with an L."

"I don't know, Mal. It coulda been. One way to tell," said Thelma, moving to the end of the bar. "This guy, he tore a page outta the phone book. I didn't care. It's the most fucked-up phone book in town."

Thelma brought the phone book to the cops. Berger opened it and went through a few pages and stopped. "The Lexington page is missing."

Daniels yawned. "Probably just a coincidence, Mal. A lot of the pages are missing." The cop looked at his watch.

Berger closed the phone book. "Anything else, Thelma? Anything."

Thelma shrugged. "Nothing important. But this Wanda chick, she wasn't no good. She was always tooling around on this guy. That's what they fought about mainly, her in the washroom giving it to some creep. I guess this guy had a case for her."

The cops stood. "Thanks, Thelma. You think of anything else you give me a call."

The cops went to the door. Thelma called out: "Hey wait. I got it." The cops turned. "The guy's nickname. Killer. That's what it was. You know, like that rock-'n'-roll jerk back in the fifties, the geek who married his ten-year-old cousin. You ain't that old, Mal, you remember him. The Killer, he called himself."

"Yeah," said the cop. "I remember him."

The cops rode in silence. Mal Berger didn't care that his partner wanted to quit. Daniels was a family man. He had that to worry about, and he was leaving the force next summer, two years early, he was fighting for a full pension and losing. And he had five hundred on the Sunday Jet game, Jets with just three and a half points, when half the bozos in town were giving Jets and six. Dan had a lot on his mind, he didn't have time to worry about his partner's screwball theories. But that was all right with Mal Berger. He wanted to work on this one alone. Off the record.

Daniels drove the unmarked car to the downtown station. He stopped in back, with the motor running. Daniels yawned. He looked at his watch. "What do you want to do, Mal? You want to follow up on this or you want to call it a night?"

Berger yawned. He checked his watch. "Let's knock off. I'm beat, Dan. Let's see what things look like in the morning."

Daniels relaxed. "Probably a good idea. Things will look better in the morning."

"I'll check the car in, Dan. Do me a favor. Pop in and tell them to keep that fucking Mehring on ice as long as they can."

Daniels looked at his partner. "If you're staying out, Mal, I'm staying with you."

"Nah, I'm coming in. Get a good three or four, Dan. See you in the morning."

Daniels got out of the car. He slapped the car roof and went into the station. When he was gone, Berger turned the car and drove away.

Mal Berger drove through the dark, empty city. Berger liked to work this time of night. The early people were all gone now, gone home, to their motels, their flophouses, wherever early people went. They were all gone but the ones the cop wanted. Berger didn't hunt, he hadn't hunted since he was a kid in Pennsylvania. He hadn't been in the woods since the war, but if he did hunt he would want to do it like this. Late in the season, when the leaves were all gone, when the trees were bare and the ground was blanketed with snow, when all the early birds were home by the fire writing checks to the taxidermist. Berger would want to hunt when there was nobody there but him and what he was hunting. When the animal could see him just as he saw the animal. Nobody else in the woods but the two of them.

Mal Berger drove away from the sea and the beaches and the city, toward the old parts of town and beyond that the redneck shacks and beyond that the swamp. It was four, still pitch-dark, but Mal Berger had no trouble finding the way through the lonely streets of the rich. He forgot faces,

he forgot names and numbers and birthdays, he forgot the
good times along with the bad, but Mal Berger never forgot
his way to a place once he had been there, not even if he
had been away twenty years. You put him in Korea tonight
and he could find division headquarters in the dark, every
place it had ever been.

Berger turned the car and went along the narrow,
winding street toward the Racicot mansion. He saw the red
cab parked where it had been earlier. Berger cursed under
his breath. They must have sprung Mehring already. He'd
come back to finish what he had started, generally fucking
up everything he could get into. Berger pulled the unmarked
car behind the cab. He left the headlights on and studied
the cab. Berger looked at the numbers on the back of the
cab—the license plate, the cab ID. He couldn't remember
the numbers from before, he didn't have the head for it, but
he knew the numbers were different. It was a red cab, just
like Mehring's cab, the cab that had been here before, but
it was another cab.

Berger switched off the headlights. He took a small
flashlight and got out of the unmarked car. He unbuttoned
his jacket and loosened his tie and took out his revolver and
went forward to the cab. Berger shined the light inside the
cab. Nothing. He played the light along the dash, on the
visor. He reached in the cab and turned up the visor. The
dead cabbie's picture and ID. He switched off the light and
looked toward the mansion. He could see a faint light
through the hanging moss and trees. Whoever the killer was
he was here.

Berger went through the trees toward the light. At one
point he crossed the gravel path that went from the road to
the house. The scrape of gravel under his feet startled him.
It came to him so loud and distinct that it seemed another
man was walking in the dark beside him. He stepped off the

195

path and stayed on the grass. Berger went through the trees uneasily. His fear of the open returned to him. He remembered why he had become a cop. A city cop. How glad he had been to leave the army, hunting and being hunted in the wild. An alley, a dark hall, a room beyond the room he had come to, these things held no terror for him. But here, among the trees, he had to fight back his fear. He went quickly over the grass toward the house. Where he knew how to stalk and kill.

Berger went up the wide steps and crossed the colonnaded porch. He pressed the door. It went back and he stepped into the house. The entry hall he had come into was dimly lit from the back. The door beneath the spiral stairs was slightly ajar and showed a slice of mustard light. More light came from the floors above, at the head of the stairs. This light fell across the stairs so that the stairs looked like the ribs of a fossil skeleton. Before the double doors that opened to the large rooms off the hall had been closed, but they were open now and dim light came from these rooms. Outside, in the dark, he had not seen it, but dawn was coming. Every window in the house showed gray.

Berger went two steps into the hall and stopped. His hard-heeled shoes cracked against the marble floor. He bent and untied his laces and stepped out of his shoes. He took off his jacket and hat and tie and loosened his collar. He listened. Nothing. Still he waited, letting his eyes adjust to the dark, till the light from the door beneath the stairs and from the upper story and from the windows in the flanking rooms grew no clearer. When he could see as well as he ever would, he went into one of the larger rooms off the hall.

The sound and the movement came to him together. They were wrong. The sound was a creak, a foot being placed on a wooden floor, but it came from above, from the ceiling. Berger looked up and saw the man hanging from the ceiling. In the dark the man seemed to be standing on his head on the ceiling. The sound came again, the rope around the man's neck straining against the ceiling beam as the man's body slowly turned.

Berger waited till he saw or heard nothing else in the room or in the hall behind him or from the room beyond the hall. Then he went to the body and switched on his light and swept the light up the body to the man's head. The man hung from the beam like a bird caught in flight, his arms and hands and fingers extended. Berger knew who the man was, the freak Lexington, but still he did not recognize the man at first, his face was so contorted from strangulation. Berger lowered the flashlight from the twisted face. The killer had killed what he had wanted to kill. Berger switched off his light and stood in the dark. That part of it was over.

Berger went into the hall and listened. Nothing. He went to the room across the hall. Nothing there. Berger came back into the hall. He went to the foot of the stairs. A sound came from above. A man's voice speaking, a gentle rush of words, like a prayer, so low and hurried Berger could not make out its meaning. Berger spoke and the voice stopped and Berger knew it was not the man he wanted. Now that there was silence Berger heard another sound, a mechanical sound coming from the door beneath the stairs, from the rooms at the back of the house.

Berger went along the hall behind the stairs. There were closets and pantries and storage rooms off the hall. Berger searched them all as he went, though he knew the killer was not there. He came to the door at the end of the hall and pushed it back. There he saw a large dark room, the kitchen, its walls hung with steel instruments and utensils and implements. There in the center of the room was a chopping block, a cleaver standing by its blade in the wood. A bank of stoves, great dark furnaces, made the kitchen's back wall. To one side of the stoves was a long table, polished white and bare as an operating table. Chairs were placed around the table. In two of the chairs sat white figures, slumped over the table. Berger worked the light switch inside the door, but the room remained dark. The cop was drawn to the figures slumped over the table at the far end of the room. He wanted to go to them now, to see how they had died, but he went inside the door and searched every part of the room as he went through it.

Something in Berger turned cold, something icy spread through him when he came close and saw the figures at the table. They were a man and a woman, the servants he had seen earlier, still dressed in white. Both had been strangled. Berger had not known such cold since the war, when an entire army had turned and fled a mindless, soulless enemy. The man had found and killed what he wanted. And he was still hunting and killing.

Berger reached up to the light suspended over the table and pulled the cord. The light did not come on. Berger saw that the bulb had been broken, crushed in its socket. He went to a wall fixture and saw that that bulb had been broken in its socket and another, it had been crushed too. Berger heard the sound again, the mechanical whine, it came from beyond a door that Berger had not noticed before, a door hidden behind the black ovens. Berger went around the table, past the ovens to the small door. He turned the knob and the door swung open. The door and the stairs leading down were miniatures, as in a child's playhouse. Mal Berger had to stoop to go through the door. Berger went down the stairs carefully, their risers were so narrow. At the foot of the stairs he saw he had come into a wine cellar, a long low-ceilinged room spread with dust and mold and dark. A light was on at one end of the room, blocked from view by the walls of wine racks that ran the length of the room. The sound, the metallic grinding, came from there, from the lighted part of the cellar. Berger chose one of the narrow walkways that ran between the wine racks and went toward the light.

As Mal Berger went between the walls of dusty, molded wine bottles he lost his sense of direction. He could not tell where the sound came from. It had been near the light or beyond it when he had stood at the foot of the stairs, but now as he went between the wine racks, the sound moved. Now it was to one side, now, as he neared the end of the walkway between the wine racks, it seemed to be behind him. Now that he came to the lighted area of the cellar—a cleared area with a small table and chairs placed beneath the light—the sound again came from the distant end of the cellar, from beyond the light. And now, as Berger stepped into the cleared, lighted area, now the sound stopped.

Berger spoke to the man waiting in the dark. He did not know what he said, whether he pleaded with the man to quit or said a name or if he said any words at all. He spoke and then listened as the sound went around the low dim room, circling him. Berger turned. He turned left and he turned right. He turned back to the way he had come. He turned a full circle and he saw and heard nothing. The sound had stopped. Berger spoke again. There was nothing but the echo of his own voice. Nothing but his shadow spreading out from the light over his head. Now Berger heard the high mechanical whine again, coming from behind him, and the man came out of the dark for him.

Berger knew the man. He knew the huge hard hands at the back of his neck and the rope they held. He was ready for the hands and the rope when they came. When the man had come at his back and the rope had gone over his head Berger had slammed his chin to his chest. He had pulled up his shoulders and hardened the muscles of his neck, so that

199

the rope had caught his chin and not his larynx and Berger could breathe as he slammed his back and the man fixed to it against the wall, the wine racks, against the wall again, punishing the man terribly for fixing himself to his back. The cop and the man on his back went around in a furious circle, racks and wine bottles overturning, bottles smashing, wine flying over the struggling men. The cop saw a jutting corner in the wall, a sharp edge, and he flung himself and his attacker around and he went backward into the sharp corner. He beat the man at his back against the corner. Again and again and again, the cop slammed backward against the corner. And then something broke within the cop. It was not his jaw that broke first. It was something deep within him. Something weak, that he had known was there all his life, that he had spoken of to no man or woman. Something secret in the cop snapped, as his jaw would snap later.

The strength was going from the cop, it was going to the man at his back. Berger could no longer strike the man's back against the sharp corner. He could only stand. He reached back with his hands, behind his head, and dug his fingers into the head locked behind his. But he had grown too weak to find the man's eyes or nose or mouth. It was as if the head behind him was faceless. The cop's weakening fingers could find nothing there to dig into, to rip out, to destroy. His fingers went to the rope, to the sides of his neck. He tried to sink his fingers between the rope and his neck but he was too weak. The rope had already cut deep into his flesh and his fingers dug into nothing but the bloody trench the rope had cut into his neck. Now the cop felt his teeth move apart. He could not keep them together. His mouth was being torn open. The rope that had caught around his chin rather than his larynx, that was digging deep into his neck, now the rope began to tear away at the muscles of his jaw, pulling his jaw down and back, breaking his jaw from his face and pulling it back into his larnyx and the soft part of the throat, strangling him.

Mal Berger's jaw was ripping backward through his throat, he was strangling on his own blood. He no longer breathed. He was growing weak and warm and soft. His sight was dimming, darkness was coming over him. The light above his head grew faint and then it went out. But Mal Berger reached into the darkness where the light had been. His hand went out and he felt the light's warmth, like the warmth that had spread everywhere now. With his last bit of strength Mal Berger took the light and he broke it in his hand. He crushed it and after he had broken the light he drove his fingers deep into its warmth. He pushed his hand, his arm, his body into the warmth, for he knew that there was life there. But it was too late for Mal Berger. By the time the electricity surged through his body, bucking his killer off his back and freeing him, by then Mal Berger was dead.

EIGHTEEN

THE cops came in the early-morning hours and took Sid Mehring from his cell. The cops and Sid Mehring went along a hall to the property desk. There Sid Mehring was checked out of jail. The clerk went through the list of Sid Mehring's property. A wallet with various credit cards. A penknife. A money clip. A wristwatch, a make the clerk had read about somewhere. The clerk asked Sid how much it had cost. Sid said he didn't have a clue, it had been a gift from his chauffeur. The clerk handed Sid Mehring his last piece of property: eighteen hundred dollars and some change in cash.

Sid Mehring pocketed his property and was led to the booking room. A sleepy young lawyer with neatly trimmed hair and rimless spectacles and clad in a jogging suit was seated at a table filing papers in an attaché case. He stood when Sid came into the room.

"I'm very very sorry all this happened, sir," said the lawyer.

"Finley?" said Sid.

"Yates, sir. Gerald Yates. Mr. Finley asked me to come down."

"Did he?" Sid looked around at the jailers. "Am I free?"

The jailers looked toward the booking clerk. The booking clerk said, "Sign here."

Sid signed the papers and the lawyer and the booking clerk each took a copy.

"You're released now, sir," said the lawyer.

"Good. What did you say your name is?"

"Gerald Yates, sir."

"Gerry, I'd like to borrow your car. I've got some errands to run." Sid reached into his pocket and drew out a bill. "You won't mind taking a cab home, will you?"

The young man looked at the hundred. "I'm afraid the driver won't have change for this, sir."

Sid took out another bill. "This should take care of it."

Sid Mehring pulled the borrowed car behind the unmarked cop car. The red cab was parked beyond, in front of the unmarked cop car. Sid did not notice that the unmarked car was Berger's, the car that had taken him to the station. He did not notice that the red cab was a different cab from the one that had brought him to the Racicot mansion. Sid Mehring scarcely noted that the red car was a cab at all.

Dawn had not yet come, but the sky was gray and Sid

could see the chalky bulk of the Racicot mansion through the trees and the hanging moss. He went to a broad gravel path and walked briskly along it, the heels of his shoes grinding into the gravel as he went. Sid noted that a drape parted in one of the second-story windows, that someone was watching him approach. Sid mounted the broad steps that fronted the mansion, went across the porch and pushed back the front door. The double doors that flanked the entry hall had been closed now and Sid went past them, the heels of his shoes cracking against the marble floor. He ran up the stairs, two at a time. At the head of the stairs Sid turned left, toward the library, the room where the drape had moved. As Sid turned to go along the hall to the front of the house, a figure moved swiftly out of the shadows behind him. A sharp, metallic object pressed at Sid's back.

"All right, you! Hold it there!" a man snarled.

Sid turned and observed a rat in an oversized hat and suit holding a small pistol. The pistol looked as if it might shoot caps, but it probably didn't, Sid thought, so he stopped. "Shall I raise my hands?"

"You are a wiseass, aren't you, Mehring? Well, you ain't going to be wise so much longer."

Now that the little man smiled or snarled or whatever it was that bared his long yellowing teeth, Sid recognized him as Ashburn's slimy assistant, whatever his name was. "Everybody's here now, pal. We got a real party going. Now march!"

Sid turned and with Waldy at his back they went along the hall and entered the library.

As Sid came into the room someone opened the blinds that covered the windows looking over the grounds of the Racicot mansion. Gray light spread from the windows across the room and Sid saw that it was Felix Racicot who had pulled the blinds. Another man, Sid could not identify him,

his back was to Sid, was curled on the sofa, asleep. As Sid
came or was prodded by Waldy farther into the room, he
saw two women seated on the floor to his left, away from
the windows. The women were Margot and the girl Sid now
recognized as Jamie Simmons. Both women were gagged,
bound hand and foot. Not far from the women a body lay
on the floor. Whoever this was was covered with a sheet.
Now that Sid and Waldy had come into the room Felix
Racicot turned from the windows and came toward Sid and
the center of the room. Felix Racicot held a pistol in his
hand, as he had when the cops had come and taken Sid
away. Except for the people placed here and there, the room
was as Sid remembered it, except that Racicot's masterpiece,
the meat painting, had been torn and slashed with a knife,
strips of canvas hanging from the frame. And there were
sheets of paper, dozens of them, scattered over the floor.

Waldy pushed Sid farther into the room. "I think he
musta just busted out of jail, Mr. Racicot. I could finish him
now and it would be legal. Maybe."

Sid looked to the women again. Margot's eyes were
wide with fear. The girl's head was bent forward, resting on
her drawn-up knees, her eyes averted. It had probably been
Waldy, Sid speculated, who had so thoughtfully tied Margot's hands in front of her, so that now all she had to do
was reach up and take the gag from her mouth to speak:
"Sid, be careful. There's something happening here—"

Waldy took the gun from Sid's back and shook it at
Margot. "You! Shut up!"

Felix Racicot had gone to one of the chairs by the fireplace. On the table by Racicot sat the same bottle of green
liqueur and the same thimble glass poured out. Now a hypodermic needle and syringe rested on the table with the bottle
and the small glass. "Now, now, no need for that," said
Racicot with a faint smile, the pistol held limp in his hand.

205

"You'll excuse Officer Wald, Sidney, please. We're all a bit tense here." The man smiled disjointedly. "You see, we're all about to die."

"Sid, there's a madman in this house—"

"Hey! I thought I told you to clam up, you talky broad!"

Sid turned to Waldy and advanced, but Margot called out, "Sid, no! We're going to need him."

"Yeah," said Waldy and blinked and shoved his glasses back up his nose.

Now Sid saw Felix Racicot more clearly. His eyes were clouded, a haze came from them that Sid imagined would never lift. Racicot's voice was furry, distant, his amusement chilling: "Sidney, please, sit, here, by me." Racicot moved the gun toward the chair opposite. "I believe you know everyone here, Sidney, but my son Byron on the couch and Lex." The man looked toward the figure covered by the sheet. "Lex is dead, Sidney, so he won't be standing. He was always such a rude boy, but now he's simply dead."

Sid went to Margot and knelt and untied her hands, moving so quickly that Waldy had nothing to do but snarl at his back. Sid spoke to the woman as he loosened the ropes: "Are you all right?"

The woman looked beyond him, toward the door. "Sid, whatever you do, be careful—there's someone out there."

Racicot's laughter came to them. "Yes, Sidney, do be careful. There's someone out there killing us. Without rhyme or reason." He turned to the rodent cop. "Don't you think we have a motiveless killer loose in this house, Officer Wald?"

Waldy moistened his lips. "Yeah, well, I ain't come across any of these bodies you mention, Mr. Racicot, except for him." He gestured toward the figure on the floor.

"They said they found him strung up downstairs. Maybe he hung himself?"

"Oh, but they're here! The house is strewn with the dead." Racicot watched Sid Mehring as Sid's look went about the room, from person to person, coming to rest on Racicot's son asleep on the couch. "The pity, the shame was killing Jimmy and Marie. They were but a rich man's servants." Racicot closed his eyes and smiled. "They didn't deserve to die."

Sid spoke to Margot: "Who is dead?"

Margot shook her head.

Waldy answered, counting on his fingers, pointing to each with the barrel of the gun. "Ash. Some cabbie. Lex under the sheet there. Somebody lugged him up here. And Mr. Racicot says he's seen two more stiffs downstairs. But I couldn't find them."

Racicot spoke, his eyes still closed: "And Lieutenant Berger. I heard him die hours ago."

Waldy spoke to Sid: "I looked all over. I didn't find no bodies but Lex. Looks like he hung himself to me."

Racicot laughed. "Did you look in the cellar, Waldy?"

"The cellar? I ain't going down there."

Sid approached Waldy, who pointed his gun at Sid. Sid said, "Don't you think it's time we called the police?"

Waldy thought. "I *am* the police."

Racicot's eyes had opened. He held the gun upright, his voice had hardened: "We won't be calling the police, Sidney. The lines are dead anyway, but even so—we won't be calling the police." Racicot smiled and relaxed the gun. "No, we'll sit here among these books and mutilated pictures, sipping wine and chatting, till he comes for us. Come, Sidney, *sit!*"

Waldy snarled. "Yeah. Do what he says. *Sit!*"

Margot had gone to the girl and loosened her bindings. But the girl remained as she had been when tied, her head rested on her knees, her eyes averted. Margot spoke to Sid: "Don't go down there, Sid."

"Yeah," Waldy said.

Sid looked from Waldy to Racicot. Their hands trembled under their little guns. He looked to Margot. He had never seen her so afraid. "All right," Sid said, "but one thing I would like to do first." Sid went across the room, moving so quickly he could have taken both guns, and gave a sweeping kick to the backside of the boy sleeping on the couch. Byron Racicot turned, facing the room, his eyes muddy, fearful, locked on the hypodermic syringe on the table by his father. "Join us," Sid said and grinned and went and sat by Felix Racicot as he had been told. Margot remained by the girl, rubbing her wrists and tending to her, though as she did and as the two men talked, her eyes went over the room, studying every detail, the guns the men held, the door, the windows, the hypodermic syringe, the bottle of green liqueur and the small glass poured out.

Felix Racicot reached to the floor and took up one of the sheets of paper scattered about. He held the paper before him and spoke to Sid Mehring: "Have you seen these, Sidney? Your letters." Racicot handed the paper to Sid. "Our letters. How the avenger downstairs came by them heaven knows."

Sid looked at the paper, one of the obscene letters he had seen earlier in Ash's file. He let the paper drift back to the floor. "I've seen them."

Racicot placed his head against the chair back. He had let the gun go limp in his hand. "Would you like to hear my theory on the killer below, Sidney? The supreme irony is that I think he thinks that you are that person, the one who wrote the letters, the person we created so carefully. I think you have become his target, Sidney."

Sid Mehring looked to Margot. She had not moved from the girl's side. "You wrote the letters, Racicot? Why?"

Racicot laughed. "Yes, we wrote the letters. Didn't we, Jamie?" The girl did not move, her head still turned away. "Why did we start them? It's difficult to remember now. I believe we hated your patronage, Sidney. That's probably how it began. The arrogance of your assuming that money could bring back to life Jamie's brother, who died because of your recklessness and your arrogance."

Sid Mehring did not speak and Felix Racicot said: "But then Jamie grew bored or frightened or sickened by our game of punishing you. She experienced distaste and bowed out. But these letters, they were too precious an investment to let go. Ash saw that immediately. It was Ash, and Lex too, he saw how we could twist the letters to another purpose. That we could write letters not *to* you but *from* you—from you to the girl. Thereby we could implicate you as the mastermind behind our plan to become unbelievably rich. So that Anza would come looking not for *us* but for *you*, Sidney. But we did such a poor job of it. It was sex, I believe, that made us so careless. In the end no one—not Anza with the cranium of a shark, not the police, not even Waldy here—would have taken them for real. No one believes them but our friend downstairs. But he, Sidney, he seems to think you are every bit as vile and evil as we made you." Racicot moved the gun toward Sid Mehring. "Every bit as vile and evil as you are."

The muddy, frightened eyes of Byron Racicot had not left the needle resting on the table by his father. "Daddy, can I go now? I want to go now."

Racicot turned the gun toward the boy. "Soon, By,

we'll all be going soon. But not quite yet. Sidney and I still have some business to discuss, don't we, Sidney?"

Sid Mehring said: "You want to talk? Let's talk. So you were the mastermind behind this drug scheme, Racicot?"

"Of course. Who else had the imagination for it? Ash? By? The girl? Lex was a genius in his own way—but at this level he lost flexibility. His decisions became mechanical. Sexual. For someone so, shall we say, imaginative in other fields, he became quite predictable as an executive of crime. And too, I had the connections. No one in Colombia in his right mind would have entrusted ten million dollars in cocaine to Lex or my son or a crooked cop. And now—now that it's too late—now that I've brushed the final stroke in my masterpiece, now that I've convinced the Colombians that I don't have the cocaine at all, that it never left Colombia, now that I have pulled off the perfect crime, now some crackers somewhere are washing their overalls in ten million dollars' worth of cocaine! It's all gone up in suds, Sidney." Felix Racicot rested his head against the chair back. "It would all be so amusing if only it weren't for this madman in my cellar."

Sid made a nasty grin. "Why did you do it, Racicot? Need the money?"

Racicot's face paled and grew rigid. "Of course I needed the money. You know I needed the money, you pig."

"That's a rather modern expression for you, Racicot."

Racicot smiled. "Yes, but it's perfect for you, Sidney. You are a pig. Greedy, greedy little pig, consuming companies like mine with their tiny offerings as if they were slop. Do you remember Racicot Enterprises, Sidney? You've forgotten it, haven't you? To jog your memory: we needed cash desperately. But you had all the cash, Sidney. Then came a man I trusted, and he advised me to go public. In a small way, he said, no one will ever notice. But then small to you and this hireling, this spy, small for you was quite large for me, and this Mehring spy doubled back on my small offering and he—and you, Sidney—*you* drove my small overpriced stock down, down, till it went off the chart. You ruined me, Sidney. Did *you* need the money?"

Racicot raised his arm and reached out and pointed the gun at Sid Mehring's face, but he did not pull the trigger. He stopped, the gun aimed at Sid Mehring. The others had stopped too. Byron Racicot stopped as he had crawled onto the floor, crawling toward the door. Waldy stopped as he was about to strike the crawling boy. Margot stopped as she was about to go between Sid and Racicot's gun. There came a sound from below, a train of blows, something heavy being dragged across stairs, and beyond that a high cry, a dry mechanical whine, like steel being ground against steel. Margot went back to the wall by the girl, Waldy stepped away from the boy, the boy crept back to the couch, and Felix Racicot lowered the gun and laughed. "What a fool I am, Sidney. There I was about to kill you, when he will do it for me."

Sidney stood and then Margot. Waldy held his gun on one and then the other. But he was looking toward the door and the pounding and the cry coming from below. Sid said: "Racicot, whatever is going on down there, we need help. I'll go and I'll come back. You'll be all right here. You've got the gun. Lock the door and wait."

Racicot laughed. "No, no, you're not going anywhere, Sidney." He turned to the rodent cop. "Waldy, you're the one who's going to go. You go downstairs and shoot our mad friend."

"Me?"

"It would be so good of you."

Waldy looked around the room. He looked at his pistol. He looked at the door. He looked at the windows and the

211

grounds beyond and safety. "Yeah. Right, Mr. Racicot. Good thinking there. I'll go downstairs and take care of this guy." He looked toward the door. The pounding and the cry had stopped. "Whoever he is."

Racicot smiled. "And Waldy, I wouldn't try to run out on us if I were you. He'll only catch you if you run."

"Hey, Mr. Racicot, I wouldn't dream of running out on you. I'll take care of this creep. Honest."

"That's good, Waldy. We'll be here waiting."

"Yeah. Sure. You'll be okay here, Mr. Racicot?"

"We'll be fine here, Waldy. I have six cartridges in my pistol and there are only five of us. Run along now."

"Yeah. Right." Waldy went to the door. He peered into the hall. "I'll be okay. I'll be back. If somebody comes up those stairs, don't shoot. It'll be me."

"Goodbye, Waldy. Go on," said Felix Racicot as the rodent cop stepped into the hall. "And tell him to hurry, please. We've been waiting so long."

Waldy liked to talk to himself from time to time, usually when he was alone. He didn't usually talk to himself, back and forth, like he was two people, when other people were around. Usually then he kept quiet, except around Ash. Ash hadn't minded, he had even liked Waldy talking to himself, the conversations Waldy had between the two people he was. Waldy wished Ash were here now. Ash would have liked Waldy's bravery as he went down the stairs like a cat, creeping along, talking to himself. So Waldy was jumping and turning this way and that as he went down the stairs, that was all right, Waldy said to himself, Ash would have said it was all right to be a scaredy-cat right now, in this creepy house, with everything looking and sounding like something it wasn't. Cats had nine lives, didn't they? They might look scared, flinching and starting and yelling at things that weren't there, but cats always came back, didn't they? That's what Waldy said to himself, and he wished Ash were here now. Waldy wished Ash were here and that he were talking to Ash, instead of it being just the two of them, the two Waldys, talking to themselves.

Waldy stopped at the bottom of the stairs. He looked down the hall. Toward the front door. The door was open. Gray light showed through it. But not that much light, just a block of gray and mist set in the dark. He could run for it now, run through the gray square of light, and he would be free and safe. Maybe. And maybe not, Waldy told himself, maybe Racicot was right. Maybe running from whatever it was that was out there hunting them was the wrong thing to do. Maybe the killer was like a barking dog. If you turned your back on him, he would come at you. But if you faced him, faced him down, he would probably just turn tail and cower and hide and give up. Waldy gazed into the dark. You had to remain the hunter in this game. You become the hunted and your goose was cooked, Waldy told himself, looking toward the open front door. And anyway it didn't look all that light out there beyond the door. It still looked, in fact, pretty dark out there.

Waldy was standing in the hall, looking at the gray open door, thinking about throwing down his gun and running through the door and the pale gray light and the trees, running as far and as fast as he could, nobody could ever catch Waldy when he was really running in his creepers, when he heard the sound again. It came from the back of the house. A high mechanical whine. It sounded just like a machine that was overheating, run low on oil or water or whatever it was that kept machines quiet. Waldy laughed out loud and said to himself that was just what the sound was. Some kind of machine. That's what it was, the servants

213

back in the kitchen, running some kind of machine, some kind of meat grinder maybe. That was the reasonable explanation Waldy was looking for. Everybody's nerves were on edge, with Lex hanging himself and Ash being dead and the cabbie too and the pilots. They were all dead, sure, but the rest of it was all in their heads. In Racicot's head mainly. The old guy was flipping out, the Colombians having reserved a car trunk for him and his son. Now the sound stopped and there was something else, a low chugging noise, muffled and quiet. There you were. A meat grinder and a blender or juicer for orange juice, they were the mechanical whine. And the low chugging, that was somebody chopping onions or carrots or something. And the train of thuds earlier, that had been somebody dragging a sack of spuds up the cellar steps. There was nothing else to it, Waldy told himself, but a bunch of good and loyal servants making an early breakfast for their master and all his friends who had happened to drop by unannounced.

Waldy went through the door under the stairs and down the long pantry hall. Waldy came to the kitchen, where the muffled chugging came from. It sounded like some kind of sobbing now, somebody crying, that was how your ears could play tricks on you. Waldy stopped and listened to the sobbing or chopping or whatever it was. He pushed open the door and peered into the kitchen. He had never felt better in his life. There they were, the four servants, all gathered around the servants' table having a bite before they served their masters. Waldy stepped into the kitchen and went toward the servants. Naughty servants, tired servants, they all had their heads down on the table, taking a little nap there on the table, like children at school. Waldy went along quiet as a mouse on his creepers, so that he wouldn't wake the servants, all sleeping but the one servant who was making the sobbing sound. That servant's head was down too, like the others, but he wasn't asleep. No, that servant was crying like a little child, as if he had had a bad dream.

Waldy came to the table where the four people sat and he saw that they weren't sleeping. They were dead. Their faces were twisted and swollen from the ropes tied around their necks. There were a man and a woman in white, they had been strangled and were dead. And there was another man, a big guy, Waldy didn't recognize him at first, his face was so mutilated and destroyed, his jaw torn away from his face. That was Lieutenant Berger and he was dead. There was the fourth figure at the table. He had his head down like the others, but he wasn't dead. He had his head on the table and he was crying.

Waldy stopped and when he stopped his creepers made a squeak on the floor, like a mouse caught in a trap, and the fourth figure at the table raised his head and looked at Waldy. Waldy thought it was an Indian at first, some Apache or something on the warpath. The man's face was streaked and painted, but then Waldy saw the man's face had been clawed and torn, and the streaks of warpaint, they were blood. The man raised his head and looked at Waldy and said something Waldy didn't understand. Waldy looked hard at the man, like the man was looking at him, except the man didn't really seem to be looking at Waldy. He wasn't seeing him. His eyes were on Waldy, but they didn't seem to care who he was or what he was doing here. They were just eyes and there weren't any tears or any unhappiness or anything at all in them. They were just eyes and they were fixed on Waldy, without curiosity or interest or care.

The man spoke again and still Waldy couldn't understand what it was he said. A single word, a name maybe. He was telling Waldy who he was and Waldy said what? or come again? or who are you anyway? Something like that.

215

The man raised his hands and Waldy saw he held a rope or a piece of string or wire or fishing line between his hands. The man said the word again. It sounded just like he said Lex, but that couldn't be, Waldy told himself and maybe he told the man, Waldy wasn't sure if he was talking aloud or to himself now. That couldn't be, Waldy said to himself and maybe the man, Waldy couldn't be Lex. Lex was dead.

Now that Sid Mehring saw Felix Racicot clearly he saw he was mad. The man's blurred eyes were uplifted, to the ruined painting, but he did not see its ruin, the canvas in tatters, torn and rent. Felix Racicot saw the painting as it had been before, when it was whole. "He was a simple man really," said Felix Racicot. "Saintly. He lived such a simple, saintly life. He loved two women—that was his only aberration. You and I, Sidney, are so much more complex. We cannot conceive of anything so pure as loving two beings with all our soul. No, our loves, and our hatreds, are tarnished and torn and spoiled. We know only complexity. Shatterings. Explosions. Witherings." Racicot reached for the small glass on the table and held it to the painting and smiled. "I think our friend below must be like an artist. His hatred of us has the simplicity of art." Racicot raised his eyes to the ruined picture. "I wonder what they would have thought of one another—the madman and the artist?"

Sid shifted, his eyes on Racicot and the gun limp in his hand. "I don't think he much liked the painting."

Racicot looked at Sid directly, puzzled for a moment, then he smiled. "Oh no, Sidney, the madman below hasn't been up here yet. He didn't destroy the painting." Racicot's gaze returned to the torn canvas. "No, another madman destroyed a thing that should have lived forever." Racicot smiled at Sid Mehring. "You see, Sidney, there's a madman loose upstairs as well."

Sid moved in the chair. "Is there? Who is that?"

Racicot laughed and raised the gun. "Sidney, you're patronizing me. Don't patronize me, Sidney, or I will shoot you."

Racicot moved the gun away from Sid Mehring. "No, I won't shoot you, Sidney. If you patronize me again—or make some sort of foolish leap for this gun—I'll shoot the woman." Racicot smiled. "Now, you'll stay in your place, won't you, Sidney, and talk some sense to a fellow rich man."

Sid moved back. "What do you want to talk about?"

Racicot looked around the room, from By cowered on the couch, to the two women sitting on the floor by the back wall. "Let's talk about being rich, Sidney, and being poor."

"All right. You start."

Racicot laughed. "I think there is only one kind of poor man, Sidney, a man who was born poor. It is quite as simple as that. Take you or me and take our money away from us and we are still rich. We were born rich. But if you gave a poor man our money or let him earn it or find it or steal it, he is not really rich. Not like us. He is merely not poor. No, one can never become rich, Sidney. To be truly rich—as you and I are rich—it is not a thing we have done. It is what we are. To be rich is a crime, of course, but it is not a crime of doing. It is a crime of being. Of existing. That is why the madman below demands our extinction. He knows the folly of taking our money from us. We will still be rich. And he will merely be not poor. No, he knows the only punishment for the crime of wealth is death. Then we are not rich any longer, Sidney."

Sid moved in the chair. Racicot did not notice the

movement. "I don't know, I bet we could buy this guy off, Racicot, if we put our minds and our assets to it."

"Oh, you would like to think so, wouldn't you, Sidney? But no, you'll never buy him. He is pure. I can feel his hatred even now. It is perfect. Without flaw. He is nearly unique in this world, I think. He is as pure below as I am pure above him. The man who loves to kill and the man who wants to die. Oh, I am so looking forward to his rope as I am sure he is so looking forward to my neck." Racicot turned to his son. "Byron, are you ready to die?"

"No, Daddy, I'm not."

Sid Mehring laughed and pinpoints of fury and sanity come to Felix Racicot's eyes. "Oh, you are going to pay now, Sidney, for being rich. You are going to pay before you die. You are going to watch all of them die. One by one." Racicot took up the hypodermic needle and stood and looked toward his son. "Byron, you must be the first. Believe me, Byron, it will be much, much easier to be first."

The boy drew back on the couch, his eyes fixed on the needle. "No, Daddy, don't. Please, I don't want to be first."

Felix Racicot stepped toward his son, the gun still aimed at Sid Mehring. "I've made up the needle just for you, son. It's what we used to put Mother down, to end her suffering. It will be much, much the best way to die. So painless and quick. You can drink the hemlock or I can shoot you or I can leave you to the madman below, but there will be so much suffering in it. I don't want you to have to suffer like Mother. Like the rest of us."

"No! No!" cried the boy and came off the couch. As he stood there came a gunshot and a strangled cry from below. The boy's legs would not hold him and he fell. As the boy fell Felix Racicot went toward him with the needle raised in his hand. As Racicot went toward the boy, he turned the gun from Sid Mehring and Sid went for the gun.

Sid struck Racicot and the gun and the needle fell from his hands to the floor. Sid took up the pistol. The boy had taken to the floor. He had crawled to the door when Sid Mehring reached him and kicked him back. Sid turned to the room and saw that Felix Racicot had gone to the table. He lifted the small glass of green liqueur to his lips and he drank. He had already fallen to the floor in convulsions by the time Sid went across the room. Now the girl came away from the wall and went toward the dying man. The bottle of green liquid had fallen to the floor and the girl took it up and pressed it to her mouth. Sid Mehring struck the bottle away from the girl. Sid knelt by Felix Racicot. His eyes were clear. He was dying, his body kicking against the poison, but it was what he wanted. Margot held the girl, pulling her away from the poison. The girl struggled to reach the bottle that was spilling on the floor. She licked her fingers, mad to die. Sid turned and saw the boy going out the door. Sid called out and raised the pistol, but he could not shoot the fleeing boy. Sid turned to the women. Margot had pulled the girl back to the wall, holding her in her arms. The girl had ceased to struggle. Now a second gunshot came from below, much closer and clearer than the first. Sid went to the door. Margot cried out his name, but Sid was into the hall and did not hear or heed her.

Sid saw Byron Racicot's body at the bottom of the stairs, lying facedown, blood running swiftly from the wound under him. Sid went down the stairs toward the boy. Then he saw the figure standing in the open door, framed against the pale gray light. To Sid it seemed that the man had been running away, but when the man reached the door and saw the light, he had stopped. Now that the man heard Sid on the stairs, he turned.

Sid saw his face. It came back to him now. The face he had seen in the cab earlier, the face caught in the windshield, looking up as Sid had looked down from the girl's apartment. Now the face was torn and streaked with blood or mud or paint and Sid saw it again. He saw it as he had seen it years ago, in a jungle, streaked like a warrior's face, with mud and blood and paint, and Sid thought of a name, a word he could not remember. Sid called out to the man, not naming him, just calling to him, and the man raised his hand and there was a gun in it. The man shot Sid Mehring and Sid fired at the man, but Sid was falling as he fired the gun and the shot did not strike the man. Sid fell forward. His body came down the stairs, striking each step in a train of blows, till his body came to rest near the boy's. As Sid Mehring was dying he saw the face come to him. He saw the blank, pitiless eyes. They did not know him. As the man went past him, on up the stairs, Sid Mehring remembered the name, what they had called the man who had killed so many other men, but he did not have the life in him to say it.

The two shots came to the women almost as one, one the echo of the other. Margot drew the girl to her and they waited, against the wall. They heard the slow even steps coming up the stairs and then there was silence and they waited, watching the door. The man did not see them at first. He stood in the door and looked about the room, seeing Felix Racicot and the dead man covered by the sheet, the window and the gray light coming through, the destroyed painting on the wall, the needle and the overturned bottle on the floor. Then the man's eyes came to Margot and the girl. Margot released the girl and stood and faced the man with the blood-painted face.

Margot wanted to speak to the man, but she could not. She raised her hands and the man came for her, coming faster than she had thought anything could possibly move.

Margot did not see his hand, but the man struck her and she was on the floor, against the wall. One of her eyes was shut and she could not open it. She could not stand or think. She saw the girl had come to her feet and had gone to the window and was crying through the glass as if there was someone beyond to help her. Margot saw the man go across the room, after the girl. He took the girl's hair and yanked her back, away from the window, and threw her into the room, tossing her from side to side by her hair, as if she were a doll.

Margot came to her feet and went after the man and struck him with all her strength. The man dropped the girl and struck Margot, once, twice, till she fell. The man lifted her by the hair. Margot could feel his face and his breath at the back of her head as he lifted her and slammed her against the wall, once, twice, till she felt nothing and her sight went dark.

Margot was on the floor, on her hands and knees. She saw the man had taken up the girl again and was striking her face and body against the wall. Margot saw the needle and syringe on the floor and she took it in her hand and crawled toward the man and the girl. The man saw Margot and let the girl go, her body sliding down the wall to the floor. The man reached down and took up the woman and lifted her to the wall and held her there, pinning her against the wall. Margot felt the man's face and breath, she felt his head pressed hard against the back of her neck, and as she was held, pinned high against the wall, she raised the needle and struck it toward the back of her head, where she felt the man's face and breath. Margot struck the needle into the back of the man's head with all the force she had left and she killed him.

* * *

221

Now there were four red cabs, three added to the first, the dead cabbie's car. The three small round men who had come in the cabs walked around the first cab, peering into it, studying it, talking low among themselves about taking care of their own, occasionally peering about, nervously looking up and down the street, looking toward the great house they could just see in the gray light that spread through the trees and hanging moss. The three men carried guns and wore caps and jackets like those worn by hunters or soldiers or bums. They studied the cab and spoke among themselves and held their guns ready and looked all about them as if they did not know what to do.

When the first shot came the three men fell to the ground and began crawling about on their stomachs. They crawled along the road to their cabs and came up behind the cars, looking toward the great house, where the shot had come from. The three men peered over their fenders and hoods and called out to one another and did not move from behind their cars. When the second and third shots came—so close as to be one—the heads of the three men disappeared behind their fenders and hoods and were not to be seen for some time. Then the peaked crown of one cap showed above the car and then the second and then the third, till three capped heads could just be seen above the fenders and hoods. The men called out to one another now, arguments, instructions and warnings, but not one of them moved from behind his car.

Then one of the small men cried out, a bleat of warning, and the three men saw danger coming from another direction. Not from the house where the gunshots had come from, but from up the street. The three men aimed their guns up the street, toward the figure coming for them. The figure came slowly, methodically down the street toward the three men. The figure moved back and forth across the street as it came, going from left to right, growing larger and larger, yet not increasing its pace. The figure, with its strange crossed approach, with its steady menacing pace, came toward the three small round men like some angel of death or vengeance or some bearer of apocalypse.

Then one of the men, the man nearest the approaching figure, called out to the others. He laughed and shouted at the two other men, their guns pointed at the poor harmless wino from Shu's delivering samples door to door. That was all their angel of death was, the first man called out, a bum out in the early morning handing out little boxes of soap door to door.

Now the three men gathered their courage and checked their guns and pulled their caps down close to their ears so that their heads were as small and round as their bellies. They would take the great house, where the gunshots had come from. They started out slowly, one man going forward from his cab to the nearest tree, then the second and then the last man darted from behind his fender and went to the nearest tree. They waited behind their trees awhile, the wino stopping on the road behind them, ignoring their warnings to take cover, standing in the middle of the road to watch the three figures as they went from one tree to the next, giving that tree a small round belly till they moved on to the next tree, approaching the house in a darting, crossing pattern like the wino had made delivering his samples.

The three small round men had come to the last trees before they reached the house, when they saw a girl's face in one of the upper windows. The girl's face had appeared framed in the glass. She seemed to be calling out to the three men though they hadn't heard her voice, it had been silenced by the glass. Then the girl's face disappeared from the window. It had gone away so quickly, so abruptly, it was as if she had never been there. It was as if a giant hand had come up behind her and yanked her back, away from the window.

The three men were waiting behind their trees, arguing among themselves, when one of the men cried out and pointed toward the great house. A woman had come out of the house. The woman came out of the front door and stood on the house's wide porch. She came and sat on the steps, looking down at the gravel path before her. The three men watched the woman. They saw she was young and she was beautiful and that she looked so sad. She sat on the steps, her head in her hands, looking down at the gravel path, her shoulders moving as if she were crying.

The three men left their trees and ran across the open space toward the woman. As the men drew near the woman they saw how young and beautiful and unhappy she really was. Her clothes were torn away from her and her arms and legs were long and curved. They saw her face was stiff and white as something carved in stone and that she held her hands to her head because her hair had been torn from her head as her clothes had been torn from her legs and arms. The men drew nearer and heard the woman was speaking. She was saying a single word over and over. They came up to the woman, till they could have touched her, and they leaned their ears to her mouth and heard the word she was saying, over and over, in a small still voice:

Help, that was what she was saying. Please help.

MAX CRAWFORD'S four previous novels include, most recently, *Lords of the Plain*, *The Bad Communist*, *The Backslider*, and *Waltz Across Texas*. A native of Texas who was many years resident in Northern California and Montana, he now lives in France.